Tales of
a Hollywood
Gossip Queen

Berkley JAM titles by Mary Kennedy

CONFESSIONS OF AN ALMOST-MOVIE STAR
TALES OF A HOLLYWOOD GOSSIP QUEEN

TALES OF A *Hollywood* GOSSIP QUEEN

Mary Kennedy

BERKLEY JAM BOOKS, NEW YORK

THE BERKLEY PUBLISHING GROUP
Published by the Penguin Group
Penguin Group (USA) Inc.
375 Hudson Street, New York, New York 10014, USA
Penguin Group (Canada), 90 Eglinton Avenue East, Suite 700, Toronto, Ontario M4P 2Y3, Canada
(a division of Pearson Penguin Canada Inc.)
Penguin Books Ltd., 80 Strand, London WC2R 0RL, England
Penguin Group Ireland, 25 St. Stephen's Green, Dublin 2, Ireland (a division of Penguin Books Ltd.)
Penguin Group (Australia), 250 Camberwell Road, Camberwell, Victoria 3124, Australia
(a division of Pearson Australia Group Pty. Ltd.)
Penguin Books India Pvt. Ltd., 11 Community Centre, Panchsheel Park, New Delhi—110 017, India
Penguin Group (NZ), Cnr. Airborne and Rosedale Roads, Albany, Auckland 1310, New Zealand
(a division of Pearson New Zealand Ltd.)
Penguin Books (South Africa) (Pty.) Ltd., 24 Sturdee Avenue, Rosebank, Johannesburg 2196,
South Africa

Penguin Books Ltd., Registered Offices: 80 Strand, London WC2R 0RL, England

This book is an original publication of The Berkley Publishing Group.

PRINTING HISTORY
Berkley JAM trade paperback edition / July 2006

Library of Congress Cataloging-in-Publication Data

Kennedy, Mary, 1944–
    Tales of a Hollywood gossip queen / Mary Kennedy.
      p. cm.
    Summary: While on a short trip to Hollywood, California, Jessie renews her acquaintance with a handsome movie star and unexpectedly lands an internship at a new entertainment magazine.
    ISBN 0-425-20993-8
    [1. Motion picture industry—Fiction. 2. Interpersonal relations—Fiction. 3. Internship programs—Fiction. 4. Actors and actresses—Fiction. 5. Hollywood (Los Angeles, Calif.)—Fiction.] I. Title.

PZ7.K38474Coq 2006
[Fic]—dc22

                                    2006042658

PRINTED IN THE UNITED STATES OF AMERICA

10 9 8 7 6 5 4 3 2 1

To Bob and Jill TenEyck, my number one fans.

Acknowledgments

I'd like to thank the Berkley team and especially my editors, Cindy Hwang and Susan McCarty, for their editorial magic and continued support.

My husband, Alan, for his computer savvy and way with words.

Siggy, who finally agreed to be photographed. His picture can be found at www.marykennedy.net

And a special thanks to Elise Monroe, who came up with the jazzy title!

Chapter One

"JESSIE, BABY, I NEVER THOUGHT I'D SEE YOU AGAIN."

That voice! It was Shane Rockett. It had to be.

The smooth-as-caramel words melted over my right earlobe, sending my pulse into overdrive and my heart dancing to a salsa rhythm. As usual, Shane had popped up when I least expected him. I was shoehorned inside an audio booth that smelled like pepperoni pizza and stale cigarette smoke at Primo Studios, a hole-in-the-wall outfit in a run-down section of West Hollywood.

I spun around and there he was, lounging against the door, giving me a slow, sexy smile, the one that drove his fans crazy. Shane looked amazing in Diesel jeans and a jet black *Reckless*

Summer T-shirt, his handsome features deeply tanned from the California sun.

"Shane!" I blurted out. "What are you doing here? I thought you were making a movie in Costa Rica with Lindsay Lohan."

He grinned, flashing a set of perfect teeth. "Lindsay Lohan? In my dreams! Jessie, hon, you must have been readin' the tabloids again." He shook his finger at me playfully. "You can't believe everythin' you read, babe. Here's the real story. I'm stickin' around L.A. all summer, just chillin' and doing some serious R & R."

"You're not working?"

"Nope. My next movie isn't scheduled until late October. Some action-adventure flick set in Mexico, with a kick-ass director who won a prize at Sundance. Gus is doing my stunts, just like the last time, but I'm hoping they at least let me get behind the wheel a couple of times. You know how I love to drive."

"I sure do," I said ruefully. I remembered my heart lodging in my throat when Shane had zoomed down the road like a Formula One driver in the indie flick *Reckless Summer.* I'd been strapped into the passenger seat next to him, my fists clenched into tight little balls as the tires squealed and the cameras rolled. The dashboard had been padded, the road cleared of traffic, but I had been convinced we were going to end up in a blazing fireball.

Shane noticed my look and his dark eyes twinkled with amusement. "I bet you're thinking of when I fired up that

Mustang convertible and tore down the highway in the chase scene? Man, that car was smokin'."

"Smoking," I said, grinning in spite of myself. Literally smoking. Clouds of blue smoke had belched from the back end of the car as Shane had jammed the accelerator to the floor, chasing a motorcycle gang out of the local diner and careening down the highway. It was one of the key scenes in the movie and would probably be dazzling on film. I missed seeing the dailies because that was the last day I worked on *Reckless Summer*, the day everything fell apart.

Shane leaned toward me, and my heart drummed against my ribs. "I'm stayin' in town for the whole summer, Jess. That item about me going to Costa Rica was just a plant, that's all."

"A plant? What do you mean, a plant?" I was still learning Hollywood-speak, and should have remembered that only half of what you read and hear in Tinseltown is true. Dreams, fantasies, and half-truths are the name of the game, and facts are routinely "spun" to make them seem more exciting.

Shane locked eyes with me. "Some wanna-be producer, or maybe his press agent, planted the piece, hoping it would get a little buzz going for his project. He figured if Lindsay and I were attached to it, he'd have a better chance of attracting some financing, and the movie would get green-lighted." There was a bitter scrape to his voice. "But as you can see, none of it was true, because I'm right here, babe."

Oh, he was here, all right. I wondered if there was a Richter scale for sexiness, because Shane's score would be off the charts. Just being close to him was having a big effect on me. My brain had turned to polenta and my heart was doing the happy dance in my chest.

"You're looking good, Jessie. So good." His voice was soft and seductive with a husky note that made me feel like I'd been torn into a million shreds. He must have come into the audio booth silently, or maybe I had been so intent on getting my voice work done, I hadn't noticed. I wondered how long he'd been standing behind me.

"Are you glad to see me?" he teased. He had an uncanny ability to read my mind and I felt my face flush as adrenaline shot through my veins.

Of course I was glad to see him. But I knew, at some deep level, that it would be a mistake to show it, and decided to play it cool. I had been caught in his web once before and vowed to be stronger this time.

Watch your step, Jess. The thought flashed through my mind like a tornado warning. I tried to give him an Uma Thurman ice maiden stare, and realized from his devilish grin that he wasn't fooled for a minute.

Shane was an expert on girls—after all, he had had plenty of practice. His electric eyes flicked over me like the lens of a camera.

"So what are you doing here?" I repeated, sidestepping his question.

"I came to see you, darlin'," he said easily, taking a step toward me. "That's obvious, isn't it? We never really got a chance to say good-bye in Bedford, you know. The movie wrapped so fast, and, well, a lot of things happened," he said vaguely.

A lot of things happened? Interesting how he glossed over the whole incident with Heidi Hopkins, his gorgeous co-star. I had caught the two of them in a major clinch and stormed away, my heart shattered. Shane had acted like it had all been a major misunderstanding and now he seemed to have wiped the whole incident from his memory banks.

I was pondering what to do next when Shane stretched his arms out, as if he wanted to embrace me in a big Texas hug. I jumped out of my seat, nervous as a cat, forgetting that my headphones were still clamped around my neck with a cord attached to the counter.

I stumbled backward, the headphones slid onto the sticky tile floor, and when I bent down to get them, Shane grabbed me by the elbows, pulling me close to him.

"Hey you, don't I even get a kiss hello?" he asked. He pulled me gently to my feet.

We were standing very close, so close I could feel the heat coming off his body, see those tawny dark eyes flecked with electricity. I suddenly felt claustrophobic in the tiny booth. There was no way I could answer him because it felt like someone had sucked all the air out of my lungs.

Without waiting for me to say a word, he bent down to brush his lips against my cheek. Very soft, almost tentative. "You have no idea how much I've missed you, Jessie," he murmured. "I flipped out when I heard Fearless was flying you out here.

Somebody in production told me there was a problem with the audio portion of the film. I was thankin' my lucky stars, I'll tell you. I drove over here as soon as I heard."

He kept his arms linked tightly around my waist, and I didn't have the willpower to pull away. In fact, I had to make a superhuman effort not to curl my arms around his neck and snuggle into his chest.

"Really?" My voice was wobbly.

"Really. I figured if you were going to be here for a few days, I could show you around Hollywood. Remember when we talked about driving out to Malibu at midnight and cruising up the Sunset Strip? I told you I'd take you shoppin' at all those little stores on Melrose? And drivin' up to Griffith Park to the planetarium to see the Hollywood sign at night? That's just the start. I've got big plans for us."

I let myself melt into his arms, turning to mush as I glanced up at him. I had forgotten the way those tawny dark eyes could look burned from beneath half-closed lids, the way his skin smelled like the sun. My heart pinged faster inside my chest as he dipped his head down to mine, and I knew that in another second it would be full-throttle kissing.

Then reality struck.

"Hey Jessie, wake up in there! We're ready for the next take!" Ron, the audio guy, tapped sharply on the window with his key ring, spoiling the moment. He was a huge, bearlike man with a red beard and a fondness for Doritos and diet sodas. He peered inside the recording booth and spotted Shane, just as I wriggled out of the clinch. "Oh, sorry, Shane. Didn't see you in there. How ya doin', man?"

Shane gave him a thumbs-up and leaned against the wall, apparently planning to drive me crazy for the rest of the taping. "Go ahead, Jessie." He motioned for me to put the headphones back on. "I'll wait right here for you."

"Ready, Jess?" Ron said, more softly this time. He shot a quick look at Shane. He must have decided he didn't want to antagonize the star.

"Ready," I said firmly. I eased myself back into the vinyl seat and clamped the headphones on my ears. "Let's do it." I focused on Ron, who was standing just beyond the glass window, fiddling with some dials in the recording studio. My hands were trembling, so I white-knuckled the mike as I waited for my cue, willing myself to be calm.

"Just a couple more lines and we're done, babe," Ron said, his voice crackling like dry leaves from the speaker tucked into the corner of the soundproofed ceiling. "Take it from the top of page six." He checked some gauges on the mixing board, working his magic, and then waved his index finger in a slow circle, motioning for me to continue.

I slapped my headphones back on and squinted at the script, ready to tackle a few more lines of dialogue from *Reckless Summer*. Somehow the audio track had developed a glitch during the shoot in my hometown in New England, and Fearless Productions had flown me out to L.A. to record my lines all over again.

I had been sitting in this cramped little booth for hours, saying my lines over and over, trying to get just the right tone, the right inflection. I'd thought my fling with show business was over. I had enjoyed my fifteen minutes of fame with *Reckless Summer*, playing opposite Shane, and I never expected to set foot on a soundstage again.

But here I was, sweaty and exhausted, my pale yellow sundress sticking to my legs, my hair trailing limply down my neck. So that's the perfect time for Shane to turn up, right?

Shane Rockett. The dazzling star of *Reckless Summer*, the guy voted "Sexiest Teen Alive" by *People*, and oh yes, the boy who had broken my heart just a few weeks earlier.

It seemed like a lifetime ago. Who would have thought Fearless Productions would come to my small Connecticut town to shoot a movie during summer vacation? And what had happened next is even more remarkable. In Hollywood-speak, they would call this the backstory.

I ended up in the movie!

Sometimes fact really is stranger than fiction, because this is exactly the way it went down. I hadn't planned on auditioning that day at Fairmont Academy, but the director picked me out of the crowd, shoved me under the lights, and bingo, I ended up getting a speaking role. In a Hollywood movie! And not just any speaking role—I was cast as the love interest for the impossibly sexy Shane Rockett.

If this was the logline for a movie, it would read: girl meets boy, girl falls head over heels for boy, boy cheats on her with a hot young actress, boy goes back to Hollywood. Meanwhile, girl's heart crumbles like a cookie. They would probably cast someone sweet and vulnerable in the role, maybe Kate Hudson.

End of story, or so I thought. But it wasn't over, because somehow Shane Rockett had found me in this crummy little studio in a forgotten corner of Hollywood.

Stay cool, Jessie, I warned myself. "I never thought things would turn out this way," I said into the mike, my voice bouncing back at me through the headphones. "I guess life is full of surprises, and I just have to make the best of it."

My voice sounded richer and more vibrant than it did in real life, and I realized Ron had probably "sweetened" it a little, adding some reverb. These were the last lines of my dialogue in my first scene in the movie.

I looked up to see Ron grin at me and make an okay sign with his thumb and forefinger before turning back to the mixing board. "That's a wrap," the voice crackled again. "Good work, Jess. Let's call it a day. We'll do the rest tomorrow." I nodded and slowly took off my headphones, replacing them on the scratched Formica counter in front of me.

I turned to Shane. "How did you know I'd be here at Primo?" I said, struggling to sound nonchalant.

"I didn't know. I took a chance. I hoped." He gave a sexy chuckle as he let his fingertips graze my bare arm, his eyes searching mine. "Sometimes my hunches pay off. C'mon, let's hit the road, darlin'."

He grabbed his car keys out of his back pocket and elbowed open the door to the booth, propelling me along with him. Shane was always moving, filled with a restless energy that came across as wildly sexy and dangerous, both in person and on the screen.

A movie critic once said that Shane always played the same part, the proverbial "bad boy" who was catnip to women. I grabbed my water bottle and backpack, sneaking a sideways glance at him as we raced through the studio, hand in hand.

"Hey, Shane, got time to autograph a few posters?" Ron called hopefully as we darted toward the exit. "I'm having a barbecue this weekend and all my nephews and nieces are big fans of yours."

"Tomorrow, man," Shane yelled back. "I've got an appointment in town." He pointed to the eye-catching Cartier tank watch on his wrist. "Gotta run, or I'll hit all the late-afternoon traffic on Wilshire. You know how it is. It'll be bumper-to-bumper all the way down the 405." He fake-smiled at Ron and gave my hand a sexy little squeeze as we zigzagged around some cables snaking across the studio floor. We were moving at a good clip, and he suddenly bent and ducked his head close to mine, his breath hot in my ear.

"Jessie, I gotta warn you. That guy is a major pest. He pretends he wants my autograph for his relatives, but he sells them on eBay for big bucks. I hate people like that. Let's get out of here before he asks for something else," he said huskily. "I've got my car right out front, and we can grab a bite to eat someplace. You don't have any plans for tonight, do you?"

I shook my head, my mind reeling. I knew I'd have to call Tracy and tell her I was having dinner with Shane.

I also knew that she'd probably kill me.

"I'll take that as a no," he said with a sly smile. "Well, you do now, babe. We've got a lot of catching up to do."

I BLINKED WHEN WE STEPPED OUT INTO THE HOT AFTERNOON sunlight bouncing off the sidewalk on West Hollywood Boulevard. And blinked once again when I saw Shane's car, a silver E-type Jag, jammed into a no-parking zone right outside the building. He tossed me a rueful smile as he grabbed the ticket off the windshield and crunched it into his pocket without looking at it.

As usual, Shane was breaking all the rules, and doing so with his usual reckless charm. Always the gentleman, he opened the door for me before racing around and getting in the driver's side.

The moment we got inside the car, he leaned over and gave me a quick kiss. His lips were soft and warm, and I had to admit the old magic was still there.

I was very glad to see him. He looked into my eyes, and I wondered what would happen next. He stared at me for a moment, his dark eyes searching, as he let his finger linger on my cheek and then gently trace the curve of my jaw. His touch managed to be gentle and wildly exciting at the same time.

"Wow, I've missed you, babe. Bedford, the movie shoot, it all seems like a lifetime ago." His voice was low and husky, and he grinned as he reached over and pushed a lock of hair out of my eyes.

He missed me? We hadn't written or spoken since *Reckless Summer* had wrapped and the cast and crew had moved back to Hollywood. Not a word. I had picked up my life exactly where it was before Shane had come on the scene. Or had I? I tried not to tell myself that I had missed him. But the truth was very different.

As hard as I had tried, I had never quite managed to completely erase Shane from my memory banks. I had missed the way his long, smoky lashes curled upward, the dazzling smile that cut from ear to ear, the sexy voice that made my pulse race. I had missed the way he made me laugh over the silliest things, the way he made me feel special and beautiful and funny.

"It was a lifetime ago," I said wryly. "If you can count three weeks as a lifetime." Had he really forgotten what had happened that day on the set with Heidi Hopkins? Or was he just putting a positive spin on things, hoping he could work his magic on me one more time?

Shane reached for a pair of blue wraparound sunglasses tucked under the sun visor and jammed a Lakers baseball cap on his head. "Gotta go incognito, as they say."

I raised my eyebrows and he looked faintly embarrassed. He had told me once he hated the whole "star" thing, and just wanted to be considered a working actor. "One of the lucky ones," he had said. "One of the two percent of SAG members who are actually employed." I remembered thinking that if ninety-eight percent of Screen Actors Guild members couldn't get a job in acting, it must be the toughest business in the world. I was glad that I didn't have any dreams of being an actress. I wanted to do something exciting and creative with my life, but I also wanted control over my career.

"Why incognito?" I adjusted the skirt of my wrinkled sundress over my knees and wished I had thought to shove my makeup bag into my backpack that morning. I knew my face looked shiny and pale after being stuck for four hours in that cramped little recording booth. A little blush and lip gloss would have done wonders for my self-confidence. This wasn't a day for the natural look; I needed some MAC magic, big time.

"Crazy fans," he said shortly. "I've gotten some weird mail and one chick is actually stalking me. She thinks we're engaged, can you believe it?" He sighed. "She signs all her letters 'yours forever.' She even sent me a picture of herself the last time. Here's the weird part." He turned to look at me, those high-voltage eyes snapping. "It was taken in my own neighborhood! I recognized the privacy hedge running along the road. She was standing right across the street from Spielberg's, which is about a block and a half from my house. Pretty scary, huh? It sounds like she's trying to tell me something, doesn't it?"

"It sounds very scary." I paused. "Do you think she's a model or an actress? And she thinks you can help her get into movies?" I remembered that Los Angeles was full of MAWs, which Tracy told me means "model, actress, whatever." Mentally, I was still reeling from the news that Shane and Steven Spielberg were neighbors, and tried to picture the two of them sharing a back-yard barbecue. Did that sort of thing happen in Hollywood? I could hardly wait to tell Tracy, who's an aspiring film director and a major Spielberg fan. Shane looked like he was waiting for me to say something, so I dragged my always-vivid imagination back to the problem at hand. "She could just be another wanna-be," I said, trying to sound reassuring. "The town has zillions of them, right?"

Shane's expression sobered. "No, that's not it. She would have sent a headshot to the production office if that's what she wanted. She's no Heidi Klum, believe me. Probably late fifties, and she's been institutionalized several times. I had a PI do a background check on her. It turns out she's hit on a lot of stars, mostly young guys on the WB. I just happen to be her flavor of the month. Lucky me," he said ruefully.

I felt a ping of alarm. "She sounds dangerous," I said. "Can't the police do anything?"

"Not until she really does something illegal, like break into my house," he said wryly. "She has to actually do something physical or at least threaten me before they can arrest her. They told me to save all the letters and if she makes any overt threats, they can pick her up. They don't have much to go on, though.

All the letters are mailed from south central L.A., with no return address and no signature."

"It sounds awful," I said. "I don't know how I'd deal with something like that."

Shane nodded. "This kind of thing happens more often than you think, but it's never happened to me before. I'm trying not to let it freak me out."

We stopped at a red light, and I noticed two girls sliding up next to us in a cherry-red PT Cruiser, eyeing Shane thoughtfully. They stared hard, a look of excited recognition flashing across their faces, and then they started giggling and pointing. The braver one started blowing kisses and waggling her finger at him in a sexy come-to-me gesture. Shane scrunched down a little in the seat and turned his face away from them.

I wondered if this happened to him all the time. I could understand how he felt, annoyed and invaded, but reluctant to insult his fans. I pretended not to notice them.

"How can you handle it? What can you do?" I tried not to look as one of the girls held up a piece of paper with a phone number on it. "Call me!" she mouthed. "Call me!"

Shane looked at her blankly before the light changed. She lifted the bottom of her T-shirt as though she was going to flash him and he quickly turned his eyes back to the light.

"I'm trying not to overreact, but I'm taking it seriously. I beefed up security, got all the locks changed, and I'm thinking of buying a Rottweiler. Maybe a couple of them." He shook his head. "Maybe I should hire a security consultant. I'm thinking about it. I don't want to wake up some morning and find some crazed stalker prowling around my living room, like David Letterman did."

I was quiet for a moment, trying to absorb this new information. It sounded like Shane was actually at risk from someone who was seriously deranged. Fear swirled through me at the thought of anything happening to him.

"But aren't you taking a chance being out in public like this, all by yourself? And driving your own car?" I asked him. "I guess I thought you'd have a chauffeur or maybe even a limo to take you around town."

Shane grinned. "A limo? That's only for premieres. I usually have my PA drive me around town, but Kevin had an audition today, so I gave him the time off. We have an arrangement; he can always go on auditions, as long as he makes up the time. So far, it's worked out okay."

"Your PA?"

"Personal assistant. You'll have to meet him sometime, he's great. He does all the boring stuff I don't have time for or don't want to do. He takes care of the house in the Hollywood Hills, does the errands, feeds the cats, handles the paperwork, things like that. And he wants to be an actor, so he understands the pressures of the business. When I've had a tough day, or just want to be by myself, he understands and gives me my space. Of course, it's a two-way street. Whenever I can throw some work his way, or recommend him for a part, I always do. He's a cool guy, you'll like him."

Shane cranked up the AC and a delicious blast of cool air danced around my legs. I felt myself unwinding, practically melting as the cool sounds of Beck drifted over me.

There was something surreal about the whole scene. Just twenty-four hours ago, I was in Bedford, Connecticut, and now I had done a complete one-eighty and was settling into the California lifestyle like a born-and-bred Angeleno. The bucket seats in the Jag were so cushy, it was like sinking into a feather bed. I stretched my legs and covered a yawn. I was surprised at how relaxed and happy I felt, just being with Shane again, feeling the excitement and heat he generated.

"Pressure?" I teased him. "You know, I think I could learn to live with this kind of pressure," I said. "In fact, I think I could learn to like it a little. Maybe I could be one of these high-maintenance Hollywood chicks I read about, the ones who spend their days being chauffeured around to fabulous lunches and spa treatments."

"Okay, there are a few perks in this business, I admit it." He laughed as he pulled out into traffic, his hands strong and tanned, incredibly sexy on the steering wheel. "And I guess I could have a chauffeur if I wanted one, but I like driving myself around, and I don't like anyone touching this baby," he said, tapping the leather-covered steering wheel.

I forced myself to concentrate on what Shane was saying, reminding myself it was all too easy to drift under his spell once again. But I was smarter this time, wasn't I? What was it they said? Fool me once, shame on you; fool me twice, shame on me. If I let Shane fool me again, the joke was surely going to be on me.

It was late afternoon and West Hollywood was bathed in a golden glow as Shane left the Santa Monica Freeway and eased into the grinding traffic on the Sunset Strip. One of the first things I had noticed about L.A. was the endless lines of traffic on the freeways. No one seemed to think anything of spending a couple of hours commuting to work. Very different from Bedford, where nothing was more than a ten-minute walk away.

"So what will it be tonight? Casual, funky, or A-list?" Shane said, breaking into my thoughts. He reached over and squeezed my knee.

"Huh?" I said, sitting up straighter.

He laughed at my blank expression. He knew he'd caught me zoning out. "Where do you want to go for dinner?" he asked patiently. "We can hit the Ivy, but there's always lots of photographers. Or Morton's or Spago, but it'll be the same thing. They'll mob us going in and they'll pounce on us coming out. I'm surprised they haven't figured out a way to have hidden cameras in the restrooms."

"There'll be photographers there?"

"Worse than photographers. Paparazzi," he said sardonically. "They never give up and they never go away."

My hand automatically went to my limp hair, clinging in damp strands to my neck. "No, please Shane, not tonight. The last thing I want is for someone to take my picture. Can't we just go someplace where nobody knows you?"

"Like Iceland?" he teased. He gave me an incredulous look and I flushed with embarrassment. What was I saying? Shane was a major star—people knew him all over the world!

"Okay, that's not an option," I said quickly. "But I'm not dressed for some fancy place. I'd much rather go someplace casual and just grab a quick sandwich."

"A sandwich? We can do better than that." He drummed his fingers on the steering wheel. "I know a great sushi place," he began and then stopped, snapping his fingers. "Nope. That won't work. You're a vegetarian."

"I'm surprised you remembered that." I felt flattered and ridiculously pleased.

"I remember everything about you, Jess." He was silent for a minute, gunning the engine and cutting across three lanes of traffic without blinking an eye. Then he snapped his fingers. "I've got it. How about a little café at the ocean? Someplace really fun and funky. I can guarantee they have vegetarian food. I know they have French toast, omelettes, that kind of stuff, because they serve breakfast all day long. The owners are good people and everyone knows me there and respects my privacy."

"That sounds perfect," I agreed.

"It's right on the boardwalk in Venice," he went on. "We can sit and stare at the ocean, or just watch the world go by. No pressure, no photographers, and no raw fish."

"You convinced me." I smiled at him.

"But you promise you'll let me take you someplace really special tomorrow night, right? There's a new club opening up on the Strip and I think I got an invitation to some benefit up at the Getty. Or there's a premiere for an indie flick down in the Valley. We can pick whatever you want."

Shane told me once that he got fifteen or twenty invitations a week to film premieres, gallery openings, charity functions, fund-raisers, and publicity events. Some stars went to everything, but he turned down most of them, picking the events that interested him, and sometimes his press agent made the selection. "You're very popular," I had teased him.

"It's not a question of being popular," he had shot back. "It's all about money."

It was true. Shane's presence at an event—a restaurant opening, for example—guaranteed media attention and created a whole new layer of buzz for the establishment. Business would soar for weeks afterward as the tourists were drawn like flies, hoping they would spot him there again. People would do anything to talk to him, touch him, spend a moment with him.

He wants to see me tomorrow night? My heart drummed against my ribs. Tomorrow was my last night in L.A. Fearless Productions, a chintzy outfit, had flown me out just for the weekend, assuming I would work on the audio track both days, with no downtime. The plan was to wrap up the looping at Primo in the morning, spend some time with Ellie in the afternoon, and then fly back to Bedford the following day.

But now all bets were off, because Shane was on the scene. I was torn. Did I really want to spoil the evening and tell him I'd be leaving the day after tomorrow? I decided to keep the illusion and live in fantasy land for a few more hours. The thought of saying good-bye to Shane—again—was just too much to deal with.

"It's up to you, babe. You're calling the shots." He flashed that familiar high-voltage smile at me as he nosed into a parking spot just a few steps away from Venice Beach. As he leaned forward to unhook his seat belt, I caught a whiff of a subtle, spicy cologne. Shane smelled delicious. He was delicious!

Suddenly, I felt free, adventurous, excited to be in California with Shane. I decided to enjoy the moment and not worry about the fact that the clock was ticking on our time together.

"Sounds great," I told him. "Anything we do together will be fun."

Chapter Two

★

I WAITED UNTIL WE WERE SEATED AT A LITTLE WROUGHT-IRON patio table before I told Shane that Tracy had come to Hollywood with me.

"Hey, that's great," he said, nodding enthusiastically. "If I had known, I would have invited her to come along with us tonight." Shane didn't look the least bit uncomfortable at the mention of Tracy, but I reminded myself that he was a trained actor, an expert at hiding his true feelings under a smooth veneer. Who knew what lurked behind that electric smile and the tawny dark eyes?

Shane had met Tracy during the filming of *Reckless Summer*, back in Bedford. Shane and I were both acting in the movie, and Tracy was doing a video diary on the production for a class project. Tracy had distrusted Shane from the get-go, warning me that he was a guy on the make, a "player," but I never knew if he sensed her dislike. She was one of the few people who wasn't caught up in the "Shane fantasy machine," as she called it.

"So, do you like my choice for dinner?" he asked, breaking into my thoughts. "Good atmosphere, right?"

"I love it," I said enthusiastically. The best part was the fact that no one was staring at him or pestering him for an autograph. For once he could relax and just be Shane, my date for the evening, not Shane Rockett, the hottest star on two coasts.

The Beach Café was a little place with a bright green awning right on Ocean Front Walk. As Shane had promised, it was funky-casual, a burger joint that offered pancakes and scrambled eggs all day long, along with vitamin-packed power drinks, which seemed to be the state drink in California. The specials were listed on a chalkboard at the entrance: mozzarella sticks, lentil soup, spaghetti and meatballs, vegetarian pizza.

Shane sat with his back to the boardwalk, hoping to discourage the tourists and gawkers who seemed to be out in full force. Ocean Front Walk was lined with T-shirt shops and funky little clothing stores and pizza joints. People were walking their dogs and pushing their kids in strollers, while a guy in a turban played an electric guitar, zipping along on his in-line skates. Street vendors hawked cheap watches and sunglasses, lining up their wares on trestle tables, calling out to passersby.

Shane took a quick glance over his shoulder before peeling off the baseball cap and running his hand through his sun-streaked blond hair. It was very sexy, a little longer than he had worn it in Bedford for the *Reckless Summer* shoot. "So where are you guys staying? Did Fearless put you up at the Beverly Wilshire?"

"The Beverly Wilshire? You've got to be kidding." I knew that the famous hotel near Rodeo Drive was a favorite of Hollywood insiders. "No, I told them we didn't need a place to stay. My mom arranged for both of us to stay with an old college friend of hers who lives in Santa Monica." I glanced at my watch. "In fact, they're probably expecting me home for dinner right this sec, so I better make a quick call." Shane silently passed his cell to me, ignoring a cute waitress who gave him a blinding smile as she vamped down the aisle carrying a tray of dirty dishes. She had waist-length, tawny blond hair and a perfectly chiseled nose, and looked like she was just busing tables until her next gig as a Victoria's Secret model. I dialed Ellie's number, hoping Tracy and Ellie had already gone out somewhere for the evening.

No such luck.

"Jess, where are you?" Tracy's voice raced over the line, bubbly, excited. "You wouldn't believe the awesome clothes I got on Melrose Avenue. Ellie knows the coolest places! We got some silver earrings that are to die for, sort of chandelier-style, but not over the top. I even bought some extra pairs to use as Christmas presents. Ellie says you can never have too many earrings."

"Tracy—"

"And Ellie offered to take us back to Melrose and get some

beaded tops, if you finish up early tomorrow. They're a little pricey, but we'll never find anything like that back home in Bedford."

Bedford! I tried not to wince. Thinking of flying back to Bedford was like being doused with warm Gatorade. Talk about a buzzkill. Bedford was so remote from my thoughts, it felt like a distant galaxy. I was wondering how to administer a verbal karate chop to Tracy's nonstop chatter, when Shane caught my eye and winked. There was no getting around it, the guy exuded sex appeal.

"Ellie's going to show me how to make a Kabbalah bracelet after dinner," Tracy prattled on. "Have you seen them? They're really hot out here."

"Mmm, I noticed," I cut in. When Madonna decided to study Jewish mysticism, she'd started a major craze and now everyone was wearing the handmade woven bracelets.

"So what time are you coming home for dinner? I told Ellie you eat anything as long as it doesn't have a face." Ellie was a fellow vegetarian, a graphic artist, and a single mom whose eighteen-year-old daughter, Heather, was studying art in Italy. She seemed happy to have us staying at her condo just a block from the Santa Monica Pier, insisting that it was no trouble having a couple of teenage houseguests.

"Tracy," I cut in firmly, "I've gotta make this quick. I'm having dinner out tonight. Could you please let Ellie know? Tell her I'm really sorry if I've inconvenienced her. It's just one of those things," I said lamely.

"Inconvenienced her!" I felt my cheeks color as she added in a rush, "Yikes, Jessie, what do you mean you're having dinner out? Ellie's cooking for us! She's been stuck in the kitchen all afternoon, up to her elbows in tofu! She planned on spending the whole evening with us. We were going to have an early dinner and then walk down to the pier for ice cream."

"I didn't plan on it," I said, my voice faltering. "It's just something that happened. I'm sure she'll understand . . ." *Understand what? That I'm dumping my best friend and my hostess for a movie star who broke my heart?* "Look, Tracy, I'll explain everything when I see you, okay? Just tell Ellie I'm sorry and I'll see you guys later. Gotta run!" I could hear an exasperated intake of breath as I clicked off and the needle on my internal guilt meter swung to red alert. I knew Miss Manners would say that my first obligation was to Tracy and Ellie, but then Miss Manners wasn't sitting across the table, picking up vibes from *People* Magazine's Hottest Teen Star in America!

"Trouble?" Shane raised a cocky eyebrow as I passed the phone back to him.

"Everything's fine," I said too brightly, trying to put a good spin on things. "Just fine."

A drop-dead-gorgeous blonde undulated over to the table to take our order. She stood too close to Shane, posing with one foot in front of the other, her body twisted into a three-quarter stance, shoulders back, hips jutting forward, as if she was ready to hit the catwalk. She had paler-than-pale hair, a Courtney Love bleach job, and greeted Shane warmly, letting her hand rest just for a second on his shoulder. Was every California wait-ress thin, blond, and beautiful? Everyone out here was a babe! I nearly asked Shane if it was a job requirement, and then de-cided it was smarter to try to ignore the bombshells in their tight, Hooters-style tees and stared at the menu.

To my amazement, Shane half stood up and kissed her on the cheek, and my heart plunged like an out-of-control eleva-tor to my toes. She blushed prettily, eating up the mind-blowing smile he gave her, and I wondered if they were "an item," as they say in the trades.

"Jessie, this is Marla," Shane said a little too casually. "She serves the best Belgian waffles in town. And they come with fresh strawberries and blueberries. Unless you want to go for the grilled veggie burger—those are good, too."

Shane managed to lock eyes with her, even though she was leaning over the table, practically flashing her perfect Dr. 90210 double Ds in his face. It was like watching a hypnotist twirl a shiny object in front of a subject's eyes, except she was waving a pair of Pamela Anderson–sized, silicone-enhanced breasts. Shane must have been made of steel, because his gaze didn't wa-ver and he stayed focused on her face, ignoring the fireworks be-low. I felt uncomfortable and ordered quickly, hoping Marla would vanish in a cloud of Beautiful and disappear back to the kitchen.

"The Belgian waffles with strawberries will be fine, I'll have that," I said, overenthusiastically. I tend to smile when I'm ner-vous, and I could feel myself grinning from ear to ear as if I were from some third world country and had never eaten a strawberry before. "And hi, Marla," I added, remembering my manners.

"Pleased to meetcha." I'd seen alligators with warmer smiles. Marla let her perfectly made-up eyes drift over me for a millisecond before swiveling her head to laser-lock Shane. "Hey, cowboy, any news on that new action-adventure flick? The Pierce Brosnan property they're supposed to be shooting down in the Valley? You haven't forgotten about me, have you? That part was written for me, you know."

She had a hopeful look in her eyes, and I suddenly thought she looked young and a little vulnerable behind the edgy-cool persona. Marla cut her eyes at Shane a little warily, clicking her pen in a nervous staccato while he pondered his reply. She seemed to have a lot riding on this movie, whatever it was, and I wondered if she was one of the MAWs Tracy had talked about. Any minute now, I expected her to whip out her headshot or demo tape. Shane told me that one time a waiter had recognized him at an industry event, followed him to the men's room and slipped his headshot under the door to the stall. Apparently in Hollywood anything goes, as long as it gets you up on the silver screen.

"Oh, that property may be in turnaround, things don't look too promising," he said lightly. "And Marla, I hate to tell you, but I think they were looking at Angelina Jolie for that role. It's a very physical part, and she killed in *Tomb Raider.* But like I said, I heard it's in turnaround, anyway, so who knows what's gonna happen."

Marla looked crushed, but quickly rallied, a brave smile plastered on her face. I knew that turnaround was the kiss of death for a film. Shane had explained to me that when a production company passes on a script, it lingers for a while before it can be sold to anyone else. So if one company passes on it, then it's stuck in turnaround before it can have another shot in the marketplace.

"Well, what about the romantic comedy Plan B was doing? Or was it New Line?" She paused, leaning even further over the table. "I can do funny, you know. I'm classically trained, but I can do funny." She jutted her chin out a little, as though Shane might challenge her ability to "do funny."

"I'm sure you can, darlin'," he said in his trademark drawl. "But who knows what's gonna happen with Plan B now that Brad and Jen aren't a couple anymore." He gave a little shrug. "All the projects are up in the air—at least that's what I read in the trades this morning." I knew that the "trades" were industry magazines like *Variety* and the *Hollywood Reporter*, and that everyone in show business read them every day from cover to cover. Every morning in Hollywood started with a Starbucks chai latte and the trades. I'd glanced at a copy of *Variety* at Primo that morning myself and knew that Plan B was the production house Brad Pitt and Jennifer Aniston had run when they were still married.

Marla apparently believed in the power of persistence. "Well, can I at least send my new headshot to your office? Or better yet, drop it off at your house?" She batted her sooty-lashed eyes at him and raised her eyebrows suggestively, but Shane wasn't taking the bait.

"Oh, just send it over to the office," Shane said pleasantly, handing her back the menus. "That way I know it'll get to the right person. You know I don't have anything in the hopper right now, though. I'm in between pictures for the next few weeks."

"But things change, right?" She smiled, winningly.

"This is Hollywood, darlin'. That's the only thing you can be sure of out here. Change is the name of the game."

"Gotcha. I'll send that headshot out tomorrow. Thanks, Shane," she said swiftly. She gathered up the menus and flashed him a final smile before sashaying down the aisle to the kitchen.

"Mission accomplished," I couldn't resist saying. "I thought she was going to whip out a script and audition for you right on the spot." I knew I sounded a little catty, but couldn't help it. Was I always going to have to share Shane with fans or wanna-bes? Could we ever have a conversation without someone in "the biz" wanting something?

Shane leaned back and sighed, playing with his key ring. "Happens all time, darlin', everyone's lookin' for their big break. They're all on their way to something better—at least they hope they are. Hollywood's the ultimate company town. Anyone who isn't in the business is an outsider, so out of the loop they might as well be invisible." I remembered that Shane had told me anyone who wasn't in show business was referred to as a "civilian."

"Don't you get annoyed by it?"

Shane grinned. "I'm used to it by now. My dentist tries to slip me his screenplays, my mechanic wants to meet my agent, and the gardener thinks he's the next Ben Stiller. I don't let it get to me because I was in the same boat once myself. You do whatever you have to do to get ahead, to make connections. When I first came to Hollywood, I was so broke I took a weekend job as a giant chicken standing outside a supermarket in Van Nuys. I was paid to stand there and wave like an idiot to everyone driving down the highway." He gave a short laugh. "My first acting gig."

"You're kidding!"

"It's the truth. It's the only job I could get and I needed money to pay for my acting classes. I was studying with Boris Berger, who's supposed to be the best around for classical training, and he doesn't come cheap. So there I was doing Chekhov and Shakespeare in little theater productions by night, and flapping my wings as I handed out flyers by day. Plus it was really hot out in the parking lot, and around midday my feathers would start molting."

He gave a throaty chuckle, and a girl at the next table looked over at him and whispered something to her friend. They both were staring at him, spellbound, and one of them whipped out her cell. She held it up at eye level, her eyes flashing with excitement, and I wondered if it was a camera phone. Would I be splashed across the tabloids tomorrow, suddenly famous as Shane's new flavor of the month? Shane either didn't notice the fact that we had an audience right next to us, or maybe he just decided to ignore it, because he kept his gaze locked on mine.

"So what happened with the chicken gig?"

"Well, every time I looked around, another part of my costume was peeling off, and I could just picture myself standing there in my boxer shorts. I thought I was going to end up as an X-rated Big Bird."

"Sounds like a nightmare." I smiled at the image of Shane's bronzed, perfect body stuffed inside a chicken costume, my pulse racing a little at the thought of him stripping down to his Calvin Kleins like an underwear model.

"People seem to think I have a lot more clout in this business than I do," he went on. "Everyone thinks I can snap my fingers and conjure up an acting job out of thin air for them, just like that. I always tell them I'm just a working actor. I don't even have my own production company, and my agent makes all my deals for me." He exhaled softly. "I could be out of a job tomorrow, but no one believes that," he added, shaking his head. "Like they say out here, you're only as good as your last picture."

"Aren't you glad I don't want to be an actress?" I teased him. "I'm probably the only person in L.A. who doesn't want you to get me an audition or a go-see. I don't even have a headshot and I don't plan on getting one." It was true. My experience with *Reckless Summer* had erased any thoughts of stardom from my mind, and I never planned to set foot on a soundstage again.

Acting was a tedious, hurry-up-and-wait ordeal, nothing like the glamour and glitz you see on Oscar night when the stars traipse down the red carpet in their Versaces and Valentinos. Once I finished the looping at Primo, I had already made up my mind that I was going to say good-bye to the business. But would I say good-bye to Shane, too? That was another question.

Shane reached over laid his hand on top of mine, his flashing dark eyes serious. "I know one thing I'm glad about, darlin'," he said softly. "I'm glad you're out here in Hollywood with me."

An hour later, Shane and I were strolling along Ocean Front Walk in Venice Beach, and Shane was back in his Lakers cap and Ray-Bans. A few people stared at him with frank curiosity, with an "is it or isn't it" look, but for the most part he went unnoticed. Just another drop-dead-gorgeous guy in a city filled with them. It was obvious that Shane spent a lot of time in Venice, because the street vendors recognized him, yelling out greetings as we passed by their loaded tables and blankets.

"Hey, Shane, you're the bomb!" A craggy-faced man in his fifties was sprawled on a concrete bench, drinking a bottle of Jack Daniels out of a paper bag. He had a hatful of change in front of him, along with a shopping cart full of wrinkled clothes and a hand-lettered cardboard sign that read: "Please help me. I'm saving up for a lobotomy."

Shane grinned and handed him a few singles. "Here you go, Rocky. Get yourself something to eat, and lay off the sauce, okay?"

"You the man, Shane, you the man!"

"He's been hanging around here for thirty years," Shane whispered, grabbing my arm and moving swiftly past a vendor selling incense and henna tattoos. "He stays in a fleabag hotel when he has a few bucks; the rest of the time he sleeps on the beach—at least until the beach patrol flushes him out at sunset. I just give him a few dollars at a time. I figure that way there's a chance he might actually spend it on food instead of booze. I gave him fifty bucks once, and what did he do? He bought himself the biggest bottle of Jose Cuervo he could find and went on a bender."

"It seems sad," I said, looking over my shoulder. I had never seen anyone homeless back in Bedford, and it seemed strange to think of it happening in this magical spot where dreams came true and every story had a happy ending.

"It's a real bummer. Rocky came out here to make his fortune and the industry chewed him up into little pieces and spit him out. If he makes it a few more years, he'll qualify for the actors' home for the aged, but I wouldn't put money on it, the way he's belting back the booze." He paused, looking out at the Pacific, which was clear and flat, a crystal aquamarine color. "There's a lesson here, you know. Never let any of this become too important to you." He turned and gestured to the wide expanse of boardwalk, the string of shops and restaurants and the Santa Monica Mountains visible in the distance. "Because you know something, Jessie? None of it's real. It's all make-believe, darlin', every single bit of it. All make-believe."

"Some of it's real, though, right?"

He grinned, knowing exactly what I meant. "Oh yeah, some of it's very real. Like this, for example." He dipped his head to brush a stray lock of hair out of my eyes and then lightly kissed me on the lips. He let his fingers graze my cheek for a second before pulling back to look at me, his dark eyes flashing. "So what would you like to do tonight, darlin'? Cruise along the Sunset Strip, or zip down to Marina del Rey to check out the yachts? Or we could drive up to the Griffith Observatory and you can get a 360-degree view of Hollywood."

He played with a strand of my hair and I rested my head on his chest for a moment, letting the warm smell of him waft over me. My whole body tingled when I was close to him and every sensation seemed magnified, every emotion heightened. Colors were brighter, flowers smelled sweeter, the soft California air felt balmier on my skin. Even the music drifting over us seemed to touch me in a way that it hadn't before, the melody resonating deep within me, calling up vivid feelings of longing and passion.

Was it love, or just some sort of weird chemistry at work? I couldn't decide, but I knew one thing: now that I had experienced it, I was addicted, and I didn't ever want to be without it!

"Maybe we can just stand here forever, locked in each other's arms," I said playfully. "We'll just hold each other, all night long, until the sun comes up. I'd be happy like that, wouldn't you?" I leaned my head back, snuggled against his strong, muscular chest, as my pulse zoomed and my insides engaged in some serious bungee jumping.

"Stand here forever? No way, José!" Shane insisted. "This is Hollywood, Jess. We've got places to go and people to see." I raised an eyebrow at him and saw that he was serious, his expression taut, his dark eyes snapping with electricity. "You know what they say about sharks, Jess? They gotta keep movin' or they die. Actors are the same way, ask anybody. We're always movin', always on the go. That's one thing I learned from my acting coach," he said seriously. "You're either movin' forward or you're movin' backward in this town. If you're standin' still, you might as well be dead."

He ignored a redhead in a leopard-print thong bikini who zipped by on Rollerblades, her perfectly sculpted body swaying from side to side, her hair flowing in the wind. "C'mon, you've got to make up your mind. It's your night, Jess, I'm cool with whatever you decide. So where will it be? I want your first night in Hollywood to be special."

"I know it'll be special, no matter what we do or where we go," I reassured him. "Let's just stay here a while longer." We stopped to listen as a guitar player strummed a medley of Beatles songs, the final chords of "Yesterday" morphing into the opening notes of "Hey Jude." The music drifted sad and plaintive in the balmy breeze, and we moved to the edge of the group, leaning against a palm tree. I suddenly knew this moment would be imprinted on my memory banks forever: the gorgeous stretch of white sand, the endless blue sea, and the blazing colors of the California sky.

I felt a little shiver go through me and my eyes suddenly

blurred with tears as a lump made its way up my throat. I brushed my hand over my eyes, hoping Shane wouldn't notice the wave of sadness that had come over me. What in the world was wrong with me? Here I was in the most perfect spot in the world, with the most perfect guy in the world, and I was ruining it by having a Sylvia Plath moment. How pathetic was that? And the weird thing was that I didn't even know why my eyelids were burning and my heart felt like a stone in my chest. Was I already thinking about leaving L.A. and leaving Shane? Was it beginning to dawn on me that I'd never find anyone like him again?

Maybe I had made a mistake by not telling him that our time together was going to be very short. Maybe I didn't want to admit to myself that soon I'd be back home in Bedford. I gave a mental shrug and settled into his arms, telling myself to enjoy the moment. Shane was standing behind me, his strong arms looped around my waist, and I could feel his heart beating as we swayed a little to the guitar music.

"After we see the sights, I'd like to go someplace quiet tonight, just the two of us. Wouldn't you?" His voice was low, sexy, hypnotizing. "We have a lot of catching up to do."

I was just about to tell him that I'd like that very much when reality intruded once again and his cell rang, playing a few bars of an eerily familiar tune. He ignored it, and I turned around as he pulled it out, glanced at the number, and crammed it back in his jeans pocket. It immediately rang again, belting out an irritating rendition of "Sweet Home Alabama."

"I should have known you were a Lynyrd Skynyrd fan," I said, laughing. Shane had a good-ole-boy, Matthew McConaughey thing going with his Texas twang and laid-back charm.

"It's Kevin's doing," he said sheepishly. "He changes the ringtone on my cell every few weeks just to annoy me. The guy obviously has too much time on his hands." Shane looked down at the phone and cursed softly. "Sorry, but I have to take this, Jess," he said apologetically. "It's business."

"Sure, no problem." I moved a few feet away, pretending to be interested in a collection of sunglasses while Shane turned away, talking softly into the phone. Was I imagining it, or had his voice taken on a sultry tone, his sexy southern drawl even more pronounced than usual? I had the uneasy feeling he was talking to a girl, and then wondered if I was being paranoid. I was trying on a twenty-dollar pair of Gucci aviator knockoffs when I heard Shane laugh, that wicked chuckle that always sent my pulse into overdrive. It certainly didn't sound like business, I thought ruefully. He happened to glance my way, and for a millisecond our eyes locked, before he ducked his head, speaking quickly into the cell, his voice low and intimate.

He's talking to a girl, I thought miserably. *I just know it. And not just any girl but one of these Hollywood hotties that seem to be everywhere.*

I had just paid for the sunglasses, figuring if I was in Hollywood I might as well look the part, when Shane sidled up to me. "Change of plans," he said a little too heartily. "Duty calls."

"Really?" I tried to keep my voice level, but I could hear the hard edge of suspicion creeping in and wondered if Shane picked up on it. "What's up?"

"Business meeting with my agent," Shane said flatly. "I've been angling for the lead in a new Dimensions flick, but the producers don't think I've got the right look. They're talking about Jude Law and Leonardo DiCaprio. It's crunch time, Jess; they're gonna pass on me unless I do something fast to change their mind."

"Jude Law or Leonardo DiCaprio?" I smiled as the famously chiseled faces came into focus in my mind: hot, sexy, and intense. "Both A-list actors, as you say out here."

Shane nodded slowly, considering. "Yeah, they're both very hot right now, big box office. Leo killed in *Titanic* and *The Aviator*, and Jude, he's a megastar. He's known all over the world, and producers think of him as a real actor. A serious actor. One of those guys who can play any part, from that soldier in *Cold Mountain* to Alfie. Anyway, Norman wants me to take a meeting at the Ivy with the suits tonight." I already knew that "the suits" meant the conservatively dressed executives who ran the business end of Hollywood. And as Shane had drummed into me a million times, the movie business is all about money, and that's why they call it show *business*. Movies have to do "big box office" so producers can get a good return on their investment and keep their shareholders happy. Shane always said that the only people who can afford to make art-house flicks are trust-fund babies who don't need the money. Everybody else needs a commercial success, like *Meet the Parents* or *Moulin Rouge*, to bring in the big bucks.

"Norman?"

"Norman Kane, my agent," Shane went on in a rapid-fire staccato. "When Norm calls, I jump; that's the way it is out here." Shane sounded keyed up, a little tense and preoccupied as he always did when the talk turned to business. There was an odd jumpiness about him, a blaze of energy barely contained in his lanky frame.

Tracy was right—he was a chameleon who could change colors and shift gears in a matter of seconds. "Never forget he's a major star, Jess," she'd told me in Bedford. "His career is always going to come first, and you'll have to learn to take a backseat to it."

Shane glanced at his watch and I exhaled softly, knowing what was coming. Rain-check time, for sure. "He figures if we all sit down together, he can persuade them to change their minds. Or at least to let me test for the part or read for them. They don't think I've got the right look," he said disbelievingly. "They said they're looking for 'edgy.' Do you believe it? Edgy! I have no idea what that means, do you?" He paused, looking down at me. "Who do you think of when you hear the word *edgy*?"

"I don't know," I said slowly. "Christian Slater would be my idea of edgy. Or maybe they mean someone like Ben McKenzie in *The O.C.*," I said helpfully. "You know, kind of a loner, someone who's on the outside looking in, but is amazingly

hot." Shane frowned and I realized I had given the wrong answer. I had forgotten that all actors have a healthy dose of nar-
cissism or they wouldn't be drawn to the profession in the first
place.

"So you're saying you don't think I could do the part, either?" He groaned.

"No, I don't mean that at all. Of course, you could do
'edgy,'" I said quickly. "You could play the part any way they
want, I know you could. You're an awesome actor, and I'm sure
they'll change their minds after they see you tonight."

Shane grinned at me. "That's a much better answer." He
paused, suddenly seeing the sunglasses. "Hey, nice shades. You
could pass for a starlet, you know," he said, teasingly.

He took my arm, and we started slowly walking back to the
car. A salty breeze had whipped up from the water, and the
western sky was spectacular, a wash of gold slashed with crim-
son, orange, and blood-red swirls. It was breathtakingly beautiful, but my heart had plummeted to my ankles. I didn't want to
leave the boardwalk, I didn't want to leave Shane, and I couldn't
believe the evening had come to a screeching halt because of a
phone call.

"I just wish your meeting wasn't tonight," I said slowly. "And
I thought you said you didn't want to go anywhere near the Ivy
because you'd be mobbed by paparazzi." I tried not to let a
whiny edge creep into my voice and reminded myself that
Tracy would tell me to "put on my big-girl panties and just get
over it." I should be able to deal with a change of plans, right?

But I felt crushed and deflated and wondered if it would always be on-again, off-again with Shane, just like it had been back in Bedford.

"I meant I didn't want to go there for dinner, darlin'. This is different, this is a business meeting. I'd take you with me, you know that, darlin'. But it wouldn't be much fun for you. All trade talk." He was practically power-walking now, and I had trouble keeping up with him. So much for his dream of spending a quiet evening with me and "catching up." So much for "this is your night." I could tell he was jazzed at the thought of meeting with producers from Dimension. I knew they were one of the biggest names in the business, and that one major deal with them could propel his already successful career into the stratosphere. I could feel the tension zinging off his body like static electricity.

"I'll make it up to you, Jess," he said as he powered the Jag away from the curb, heading north to Santa Monica and Ellie's condo. "We have all the time in the world, right?"

Wrong. The clock was ticking, the meter was running on our time together, but no matter how hard I tried, I couldn't bring myself to say the words out loud.

Chapter Three

"I CAN'T BELIEVE IT! HE LEFT YOU TO GO TO A BUSINESS MEET-ING?" Tracy asked, her blue eyes round with disbelief. "First he shows up at Primo out of the blue, drags you away for a night on the town, and then poof! He's gone? That's it? Sometimes I can't believe this guy is for real," she muttered. "I'm telling you, Jess, watch out for him. He's a player, always has been, always will be." We were nibbling on nachos and watching the sunset from Ellie's balcony, which had an amazing view of the ocean and the Santa Monica Pier.

It was nearly dusk and long shadows of purple and ochre were creeping across the silky sand to the Pacific, turning the glassy sea from peacock blue to dull pewter. The famous Ferris wheel twinkled below us, and beyond the sea wall, I watched the glowing lights of tankers and container ships making their way lazily across the horizon. There was a slight chill in the air, and I pulled my new pale blue Juicy hoodie closer around my shoulders. An image of Shane sitting at the Ivy, surrounded by movers and shakers in the "industry," flashed into my mind, but I pushed it away. That was his world, his business, and I didn't really belong there.

I didn't bother telling Tracy that Shane didn't have to drag me kicking and screaming away from Primo; I was dying to go out to dinner with him! I suppose if I put a really good spin on it, I could even convince myself that it wasn't his fault our date was cut short, that it was really out of his control, but I didn't feel like making excuses for Shane.

Especially not to Tracy, who not only was my best friend, but had been my shoulder to cry on during the whole Heidi Hopkins episode back in Bedford. Tracy never misses a chance to remind me that I caught Shane and Heidi—a Britney Spears look-alike—in a major clinch on the *Reckless Summer* set, and that he's not to be trusted. Sometimes I wonder if Tracy knows a little too much about my life. One Christmas she gave me a little throw pillow that read, *We'll be friends forever, because I know where the bodies are buried.*

"So how was dinner?" I asked, eager to change the subject.

"It was fun." Tracy brightened. "Ellie's an awesome cook. She said she could spend the whole day in the kitchen, can you believe it?" She lowered her voice, glancing through the sliding door to the living room where Ellie was fixing a pitcher of tea.

"By the way, she wants to take us out somewhere special for dinner tomorrow night, since it's our last night in town. I've already told her it would be great, so I hope you're not going to disappoint her." Tracy cut her eyes at me, as if daring me to say I had other plans for the following evening.

"Tracy, that's very nice of her, but the thing is—" I began, but stopped suddenly when the screen door behind me slid open and Ellie suddenly appeared carrying a ceramic jug of green tea and a plate of almond cookies.

"I heard you say you went to Venice Beach. Did you like it?" She was thin, beautiful, a dead ringer for Kelly Rowan who plays Sandy Cohen's wife on *The O.C.* She wore her streaky blond hair hanging loose around her shoulders, and looked like a model in her raspberry boatnecked sweater and white capris.

"She liked it," Tracy answered for me, "except her date did a David Copperfield on her."

"David Copperfield?" Ellie looked bewildered.

"Or should I say Houdini? Isn't he the guy who did the disappearing acts?"

"Trace," I said warningly. I turned to Ellie and she handed me a glass of iced tea. "I ran into Shane Rockett when I was doing some looping at Primo today and he asked me out for dinner. It was no big deal, really. I'm sorry I missed your vegetarian stir-fry, though; it was really nice of you to bother."

A little smile tugged at the corner of Ellie's mouth and I wondered if she completely bought my explanation. "So Shane Rockett's in town. Funny, I thought I just heard on *E.T.* that he was off somewhere in Belize, scouting locations for his new movie."

"That's just tabloid talk," I told her. I ignored Tracy as she rolled her eyes at me, mocking my attempt to sound like a Hollywood insider. "He explained the whole thing to me over dinner. If people think he's attached to a project, it's easier to get financing. But there isn't any new movie at the moment. He's between pictures, and that's why he couldn't spend the whole evening with me; he had some big business deal going on at the Ivy." I hesitated, finding myself making excuses for Shane, as usual. "He would have come in to say hello, but he was running late."

"That sounds like Shane, burning the candle at both ends, as usual," Ellie said in her low-key way. "He has a reputation for being one of the hardest-working young actors in town. He usually schedules things back to back with no downtime. I'm surprised he doesn't have his own production company by now. I bet his mother would love that. She's always dreamed about a movie career for herself, and snared a few parts here and there, mostly B pictures. I think she always concentrated on Shane's career, and put her own career on hold so she could devote herself to being his manager. At least that's the way it was when he was growing up; I don't know what the situation is now." Ellie sipped her tea. "She's a lovely person, though."

"You know his mother?" I had seen Lily Rockett's picture in a tabloid magazine in a "Star Mom" feature back in Bedford during the *Reckless Summer* shoot. She had been standing on the Sunset Strip with Shane, wearing a sheer slip dress and looking a lot like Lisa Gastineau with her toothy smile and trademark mane of blond hair cascading down her back. I remember thinking she was so young and drop-dead gorgeous, she could easily have passed for Shane's date.

"We did a charity fund-raiser together once; she's a big animal rights activist," Ellie said simply. "Not that she'd remember me. I did the decorations and they auctioned off two of my watercolors at a silent auction after the party. She hosted the whole thing at her house and it was fabulous. She bought one of my paintings last year, but we didn't meet; she bought it directly from the gallery." Ellie was a gifted artist, and every wall in her place was filled with her distinctive watercolor seascapes and flowers.

She tucked her espadrilles under her and gestured to a pile of tourist brochures on a wicker table. "So, girls, what's on for tomorrow? We have to do something wonderful before you head back to the East Coast." She nibbled at a nacho and stared up at the darkening sky. "Honestly, I don't know why you can't stay out here longer, there's so much I'd like to show you." She gave a wan smile. "I'm lonely, rattling around the condo by myself since Heather's been away. I guess I just miss having teenagers around the house. I feel like calling your mother, Jessie, and asking her to change the plane tickets. A couple of more weeks out here would give us the chance to do some serious sightseeing."

"About tomorrow," I began, ignoring Tracy's warning look. I knew I had to speak up and confess I'd made dinner plans with Shane before she got too far with her own plans for us.

"I think Shutters would be fun for breakfast," Ellie said, naming a famous spot on the Santa Monica oceanfront. "Then we can rent bikes and ride along the promenade. That is, if we don't pig out on their griddlecakes and homemade blueberry muffins, which are amazing. This is no time to be doing Atkins, believe me," she said, patting her flat stomach. "It's going to be carb city for me, all the way." She turned to me. "And I thought we could hit Rodeo Drive after lunch, and maybe even make a quick trip up to the Getty afterward, if we have time."

"The Getty would be terrific!" Tracy said enthusiastically. "There's an exhibit of black-and-white photography I'm dying to see." I knew the Getty Center was a fabulous museum, perched high on a cliff in Malibu, and it would mean a lot to Tracy to visit it. Tracy's an aspiring filmmaker and she did a video diary of the *Reckless Summer* shoot for a special school project.

I wanted to see the Getty, too, but my stomach was churning with anxiety at the way things were shaping up for my last day in town. How I was going to juggle looping at Primo, dinner with Shane, and several hours of sightseeing with Tracy and Ellie? Ellie must have sensed my hesitation, because she gave me a searching look, her green eyes serious. "Unless that interferes with your work at Primo, Jessie. We'll make sure we schedule everything around that—after all, that's why you came out here. What time do you have to be over at the studio?"

"I think it's pretty flexible," I said, color rising in my cheeks. "But the thing is, I'm not sure about the evening. You see, Shane and I . . . I mean, it's very possible—"

"Oh, excuse me," Ellie said, jumping to her feet as the phone rang. "Hold that thought, sweetie," she said. "I'll be right back." Moments later, Ellie wandered back onto the balcony, talking excitedly into her cell. She gestured to the phone and rolled her eyes, mouthing something I couldn't quite catch. "Well, it's nice to talk to you, too, Lily," she was saying. "What a terrific idea! I know the girls would love to be part of the surprise." She glanced back at us, her green eyes widening and then crinkling in a smile. "How sweet of you to think of us. We were just talking about doing something special. Tomorrow is their last night in town, you know." She paused, listening. "Yes, I wish we could work something out, too. I love having them here, and who knows when they'll be out this way again."

I was stunned. Lily? Was this just a coincidence or could it really be Lily Rockett?

"No, I'll tell Jessie not to say a word. I'm sure she can keep a secret." Tracy and I exchanged a look while Ellie murmured, "That would be lovely, and I'm glad you're enjoying the painting. Yes, I've done a few more in the same style; I'll be glad to show them to you sometime. You could drop by the studio, or I'll be glad to bring them over. See you tomorrow, then." She clicked the phone shut and a little smile played around her lips. "Well, it looks like we don't have to make any plans for tomorrow night, girls, because suddenly we've got the hottest ticket in town. Who would think it? We've made the Hollywood A-list!"

"The A-list?"

"Can you believe it!?" She lifted her arms over her head like a flamenco dancer and snapped her fingers like castanets as she did her own zany version of the happy dance. "All three of us are going to Shane Rockett's birthday party!"

"You're kidding!" Tracy's voice was a squeak as she leapt up like a salmon, nearly upsetting her glass of iced tea.

Ellie's face was aglow. "Lily's hosting it tomorrow night, at her place. Eight sharp, and she's asking people not to bring a gift. She'd prefer you'd make a donation to an animal welfare charity instead, in Shane's name. I'll go ahead and write out a check for all of us."

"Ohmigosh, Jessie, is this awesome or what?" Tracy squealed.

"Totally awesome," I agreed, adrenaline steaming through me. Shane was having a birthday party? The impossible had happened. I was going to spend my last night in Hollywood at an A-list party, hosted by the fabulous Lily Rockett! Shane was right when he said that things could change in a heartbeat in Hollywood and go from good, to bad, to fabulous and back again.

"Wow! That is so cool! And did I hear you say it's a surprise party?" Tracy asked, shooting me a curious look, probably wondering why I was in sphinx mode. I was so quiet, I could have been imitating a mime. I didn't even know it was Shane's birthday, and never in a million years had I expected something like this.

"Shane doesn't know a thing about it, and she's sworn everyone to secrecy. She's having the party at her place up in the Hollywood Hills, and she said she's counting on us being there. I've been dying to see her house; I heard she has one of my watercolors hanging right in the foyer. Is that cool, or what? Oh, and another thing," she rushed on. "Lily said he'd planned on taking you out to dinner, Jessie, and she's going to think of some excuse to make him stop by her place and spring the surprise. So whatever he says, just play along with it."

"Do you suppose he suspects something's up?" Tracy asked. For someone who usually made fun of Hollywood and all its pretensions, I noticed her face was flushed with excitement at the thought of going to an A-list event.

"No, I'm sure he doesn't," I said slowly. "He just assumed we'd get together later in the day and go out to dinner. Just the two of us." My heart gave a funny little lurch when I suddenly realized that our plans had done a one-eighty. No intimate little tête-à-tête, no strolling hand in hand on a moon-drenched beach, no smoldering kisses under a starry sky. Instead, I'd be sharing Shane with a roomful of strangers, players, celebs, and whoever else makes the Hollywood A-list. But I reminded myself this was no time to have a pity party. Just twenty-four hours after arriving in L.A., I was headed to the hottest event in town!

"Oh, wait a minute," Tracy said, in a panicky voice. "What will we wear? All I brought is casual stuff, a couple of skirts and jeans." She turned to me, frowning at the khaki cargo shorts and white Gap T-shirt I'd changed into a few minutes earlier. "Jessie, you don't have anything to wear, either."

"Don't worry, we'll hit the shops on Melrose tomorrow," Ellie said firmly. "My treat. You both need something fabulous. This is a once-in-a-lifetime event, right?" She looked at us fondly. "Your first Hollywood party."

"THE BOHO LOOK IS REALLY IN," ELLIE SAID THE FOLLOWING AFTER-noon as we raided the stores on Melrose Avenue, a trendy shopping area in Burbank, not far from Paramount Studios. Earlier that morning, I had put in a couple of sweaty hours back in the audio booth, looping with Ron at Primo, and I was grateful to have the rest of the day off.

She led me to a rack of brightly colored separates that reminded me of *That '70s Show*. "This is a great look for you, Jess—it's young, it's hot, and you've got a nice slim figure to carry it off. I'd go for calf length on the skirt," she cautioned. "A full skirt just doesn't look right if it's too short. And go for a ribbed tank, or a soft blouse, something soft with a scooped neck."

"The boho look?" After my initial sticker shock, I tried not looking at the price tags and reminded myself that in Hollywood nothing comes cheap, not even cotton skirts and blouses.

We'd already been to hot boutiques like Madison and Tracey Ross and we'd just ducked into a new place called Paragon, where Cameron Diaz and Lindsay Lohan had been spotted snapping up the latest looks.

"Bohemian," Ellie explained. "You know what they say? Everything old is new again. The bohemian look is very retro, and it's back in style. You have to put it together carefully, though, and pick just the right accessories so you don't look like a refugee from Woodstock." She chose a beautiful Mexican skirt in swirling sunset colors and held it against me. "This would be gorgeous with one of those hand-embroidered peasant blouses, Jess," she added thoughtfully. "And some of the Indian jewelry. Not too much, though, just a couple of thin gold chains. And maybe a bracelet."

"Ta-da!" Tracy emerged from the dressing room in a soft yellow tie-dyed Indian cotton shift, looking shyly pleased with herself. "Ellie, what do think?"

"It's perfect!" Ellie pronounced. In the end, she insisted on buying a wine-colored tanzanite necklace for Tracy and a mind-blowingly expensive leather belt for me to wear with the Mexican skirt. "That updates it," she said firmly. "You look fantastic."

"You're sure it's not too over the top?" I said, after slipping into the skirt and top. I never would have picked the outfit on my own, but I didn't want to hurt Ellie's feelings. "I don't know, I'm just not sure that this is the right look for me."

"I'm telling you, it's perfect. You both look fabulous," Ellie pronounced. "Tonight, you girls will be the stars of the party."

We went shopping for shoes at the Beverly Center, which is a giant indoor shopping mall in West Hollywood, filled with upscale boutiques and designer clothes. Ellie was a world-class shopper and moved swiftly up and down the aisles, tossing out boxes of shoes for us to try on. Tracy and I finally found sexy little sandals that matched our outfits, and Ellie bought herself a pair of Chanel ballet flats. On the way out, she spotted a pair of Christian LouBoutin black satin cocktail pumps and held them up for our approval. I glanced at the price tag and my voice skyrocketed several octaves. "Ouch! You could buy a used Honda Civic for that price!"

"But they go with everything," she said, furrowing her perfectly plucked brow. "And they'll last forever because classic never goes out of style. Jessie, I am so tempted!"

"Ellie, they should come with a motor and four wheels for that kind of money." My mother's lessons in New England thrift were very much a part of me, and no matter how hard I tried, I knew I'd never get used to the wild excesses of the Hollywood lifestyle.

Ellie chewed her lower lip, looking contrite. "Oh, you're right, of course." She sighed. "Good-bye, my pretties, find happiness with someone else." She gave a pretty little moue of disappointment and blew an air kiss to the pumps as she replaced them on the rack. "So," she said, leading the way to the underground parking garage, "it's time for us to hit the road. Everyone ready for a quick lunch? I know just the place."

Moments later, we were cruising down the Sunset Strip, past

the Chateau Marmont, an old-style Hollywood hotel that was a famous landmark popular with movie stars. As we tooled past the Viper Room, where River Phoenix had met a sad end, Ellie kept up a running patter about people and places in the entertainment industry.

She was a walking *Access Hollywood*, giving us the inside gossip on the hottest stars and the hippest filmmakers. She knew all about ten-million-dollar deals, and monkey points, and who had enough clout at the box office to "open" a movie, and whose new release was on a "straight-to-video" trajectory.

As Shane said, L.A. was a "company town," and the film industry was the most high-profile employer. When you live in L.A. you become an instant expert on the movie business, and everyone from parking lot attendants to beauticians read the trades on a daily basis. Everybody has a friend or relative in the business or wants to get into show business themselves.

We turned onto Santa Monica Boulevard, heading toward West Hollywood, as Ellie hummed along to Fleetwood Mac on her high-tech sound system. I smiled to myself, thinking it was my mom's favorite group. She turned in to the Beverly Hills Hotel, home of the Polo Lounge, a famously fabulous spot where megadeals were signed over double skim lattes and power lunches. A darkly handsome parking valet gave Ellie a blinding smile as he opened her door with a flourish, bowing dramatically.

"So, Eduardo, how's it going?" Ellie said cheerily, slipping out of the black Range Rover.

Eduardo's face lit up at the recognition. "*Bueno! Muy bueno!* I'm up for a guest shot on *Desperate Housewives* next week. It's a small part, an under-five, but it's a kick-ass character, you know?" I knew "under-five" had something to do with the union rate scale, and as long as the part had fewer than five lines, you could be paid at a lower rate.

"Good luck, Eduardo. Hope you nail it. This could be your lucky break." She waited until we were out of earshot before arching her eyebrows and whispering to me, "Poor baby, he's worked here for five years, waiting to be discovered. He goes on auditions every second he's not parking cars, but he doesn't even have an agent. And you know what they say—an actor without an agent is an actor without a chance." We headed for the Fountain Café inside the hotel, where celebs gathered for quick snacks and lattes. "I'm afraid Eduardo is just another Hollywood hopeful," she added with a sigh. "The town is full of them."

Half an hour later, over grilled cheese sandwiches and iced tea, I had my first celebrity sighting. "Ohmigosh," I whispered, "is that Matt Damon? Or is it one of those celebrity look-alikes?" I nudged Tracy and we both turned to stare at the Hollywood hunk with the trademark dirty-blond hair and high-voltage smile.

"That's got to be Matt Damon," Ellie said, amused that my jaw had practically dropped onto the tabletop. "Nobody else has that killer smile." She was right. The star of *The Bourne Identity* radiated charm, even as he ordered a milkshake. My heart flooded with excitement and I gawked shamelessly at the other patrons, wondering what other star sightings were in store.

At the next table, a short, balding man was talking earnestly to a thin blonde in a tailored black suit. She could have been a *Maxim* model, her auburn hair cut in a stylish bob, a sexy peach camisole peeking out from under her Armani suit. The perfect mixture of business and sheer sex appeal. Very Hollywood.

"Is she a supermodel?" Tracy whispered. "She's a knockout."

Ellie shook her head. "That's Hildy Lancaster, the ultimate combination of beauty and brains. Her companion is the head of one of the biggest studios. She's an agent with ICM and she has a reputation for fierce loyalty to her clients and making killer deals. It's easy to underestimate her because she's so gorgeous, but she's definitely a player. Rumor has it she might be running ICM herself one day." I raised my eyebrows and she went on, "International Creative Management, one of the most powerful agencies in town."

"She looks so young." I sipped my iced tea, trying to sneak another look at the überagent.

"This is a young town. By the way, Matt Damon's going to be a surprise guest on Jay Leno tonight," Ellie said casually. "We should tape it and watch it tomorrow, it should really be a hoot. Even Jay doesn't know about Matt's guest appearance. My cousin tipped me off last week."

I stared at her. "Your cousin knows Matt Damon?"

Ellie laughed. "No, but my cousin's sister-in-law works as a marketing exec for Universal and her secretary's hairstylist has coffee with the staffer who schedules the guests for *The Tonight Show*." She laughed at my startled expression as I tried to trace the tangled connection. "It sounds complicated, but honestly, everyone out here knows everyone else. You know, six degrees of separation."

"Six degrees of separation," I nodded. "I've heard of that." Shane had already explained that one to me. The story goes that everyone in the world is connected to each other by six other people. Some people use Kevin Bacon as an example. In other words, you know someone who knows someone, and that person knows someone who knows someone, and so on, until eventually you work your way back to Kevin Bacon. So you're only six degrees away from the star himself, but it works for anybody in the planet.

"And look, there's Dominick Dunne," Ellie said. "He covers all the high-profile Hollywood trials, and writes for *Vanity Fair*." She paused. "He's also a novelist, but it's his crime and society reporting that made him famous. They say he knows the inside gossip on everyone, and he jots everything down in one of those little journals he always carries." She gave a little wave to the silver-haired writer, who gave a courtly bow before heading to the lobby.

I was surprised at Ellie's show business connections, but Mom had told me that Ellie had worked in development before quitting to pursue her painting full-time, and her ex-husband was a well-known producer, with a bungalow office at Paramount. Ellie had the gift of remaining friendly with everyone, and her show business friends snapped up her signature watercolors almost as fast as she could produce them. I wondered how much she knew about Shane, and what sort of reputation he had in the industry, but I hesitated to ask.

Ellie was bound to know the real scoop on Shane, who he was seeing, who he had dumped, but did I really want to know? Or did I want to live in the moment, and see what the evening would bring? Before I knew it, I'd be back in Bedford, and Hollywood would be a distant memory.

Chapter Four

★

"I CAN'T BELIEVE MY MOM," SHANE SAID, HIS VOICE TIGHT WITH annoyance. "One crisis after another, and of all the nights for it to happen!" After zipping along the Palisades Beach Road from Santa Monica, we turned onto the Sunset Strip and were cruising up past Mulholland into the famous canyons; Laurel, Benedict, and Coldwater. I knew this was movie-star country. We passed rows of stately mansions with palm trees and manicured lawns, and mini-Versailleses protected by elaborate wrought-iron security gates. The fantasy castles reminded me of the opening credits of *The Beverly Hillbillies*, a 1960s TV show that my mom watches on DVD.

"It's no problem, Shane, honestly," I said, thinking he had

no idea what was in store for him. "If she sounded upset, it's better to stop by the house and see what's going on."

"Here I've been over at Burbank all morning taking meetings, and playing golf in the afternoon, but she swears I picked up her car keys by mistake this morning." He shook his head in disbelief. "Why I have to go home and prove I don't have them is beyond me. Believe me, it'll only take a second. I bet I'll find them on the hall table." He glanced over at me, his dark eyes intense, and he reached over and gave my bare knee a warm little squeeze. "I'm really sorry about this, Jess. I'll call ahead and make sure they hold our reservations. You're very sweet to be so understanding." He turned and gave me an absolutely heart-melting smile. I knew he had planned on having dinner at Koi, a trendy new spot that served vegetarian sushi.

"I don't mind stopping by her house," I said in my most convincing voice. "This is a beautiful drive, I'm really enjoying it." It was nearly seven, and an apricot sun was slowly breaking through the chowderlike L.A. smog, promising a spectacular sunset an hour from now. I was wearing my new boho outfit from Melrose Avenue and Shane had given a low appreciative whistle when he'd picked me up at the condo earlier that evening. Ellie and Tracy were lounging around in jeans, planning on changing and dashing over to the party the minute Shane and I were safely out the door.

"She bought this place in the canyon after the divorce," Shane went on. "It was part of the settlement. I spent a couple of years in Pasadena, and had a lot of friends there, but Mom said there were too many memories connected with the house and she wanted to make a fresh start. It was a big upheaval in my life, but the decision was out of my hands. My father said you can make friends anywhere, but he of all people should know that it's not the same. In this town, you always wonder if your new buddy has an agenda. Quite a few of them do. You wouldn't believe how many people want to be my new best friend." He gave a cynical half smile.

A muscle tightened in his jaw, and I realized that he had said very little about his father during the few months I had known him. I read in the tabloids that Shane didn't get along with his new stepmother, Jasmine, a twenty-eight-year-old "D-girl," or development girl, at Warner's. From the closed look on his face, I knew the topic was off-limits and vowed to never bring it up with him, even though I was curious.

My own father bowed out of the picture when I was three, so I could relate to the angry vibes Shane was giving off. When you lose a parent that young, you feel as though you've been shot down the waterslide of life. The only positive thing about taking such a big hit is that usually you form an even closer bond with your remaining parent, and I think this was the case with Shane and his mother, Lily.

Before I could ask any questions, Shane swung the Jag into a curving driveway and jumped out, in his slightly manic, high-energy way. He raced around to open the car door for me and laughed when he heard me gasp in surprise. Not only was the driveway paved with yellow brick, but there was a life-sized metal sculpture of the Tin Man poised along the flagstone path leading to the house. *A yellow brick road? The Tin Man? Did somebody wish she was back in Kansas?*

"My mom loves *The Wizard of Oz*," Shane explained, giving a little shrug. He had obviously given this spiel many times before. "The Cowardly Lion's in the backyard with the Scarecrow and Dorothy's over there, staring into the Japanese fish pond."

"And Toto?" I couldn't resist asking.

"Right by her side. If you bend down and look through the rosebush, you can see him." He flicked his hand at a "meditation garden" at the side of the estate, complete with a small waterfall and a massive brass gong.

"They're awesome. How did she ever find them?"

"Oh, she didn't find them. She commissioned some artist in Venice to re-create them from old movie stills for her." He grinned. "Only in Hollywood."

He grabbed my hand as we walked past a terraced garden up to a sprawling, Mediterranean-style mansion with a cream-colored stucco exterior and a red-tiled roof. It was straight out of *Lifestyles of the Rich and Famous*, a villa the size of a small hotel complete with splashing fountain and European-style courtyard with purple and pink bougainvillea trailing down the stone privacy wall. I could see a glittering swimming pool at the far end of the sweeping lawn, and a tennis court almost hidden by banks of flowering gardenias. The air was thick with the heady smell of jasmine and orange blossoms, and I felt my sinuses start to itch, as if I were trapped inside the world's largest flower shop.

"That's funny, the lights are out," Shane said, pushing open the massive front door. I hung back a little, knowing what would happen next. "Hey, anybody home? Mom? What's going on?"

"Surprise, Shane! Happy birthday!" Shane stepped back hard on my foot as all the lights came on and the pounding rhythm of the Beatles song "Birthday" blared through a sleekly modern living room, packed with wall-to-wall people. *"You say it's your birthday, we're gonna have a good time . . ."*

Suddenly the whole crowd surged forward to envelop him in a crushing embrace, like a giant amoeba. "Happy birthday, Shane! We love you, Shane!" Girlish squeals pierced the air and the floral scent was quickly replaced by suffocating waves of Chanel and Passion as my eyes watered and my nose twitched. I was dangerously close to sneezing and surreptitiously pinched my nostrils together when I thought no one was looking.

It was the ultimate Hollywood fantasy party. Dozens of ivory vanilla candles blazing on every surface, Japanese arrangements of yellow forsythia and white cherry blossoms, tuxedo-clad waiters circulating with trays of cosmopolitans and Diet Cokes. Most of the guests were gorgeous young starlets who wore lingerie-type slip dresses and filmy baby-doll tops with tight pants.

Everyone but me, of course, who was wrapped in yards of gauzy "ethnic" fabric in the always-popular "boho" look. If there were fashion police around, I would be shot on sight. Or maybe I could just shoot myself, I thought, wondering if there was time to call Tracy and tell her to change out of her tie-dyed number into something else.

I caught a glimpse of myself in a gilt-edged wall mirror in the foyer, and my worst fears were confirmed. Surrounded by sylphlike girls in delicate pastels, I stood out in swirls of fire engine red and French's mustard yellow.

I looked like a walking piñata.

A curvy brunette I recognized from *The* O.C. elbowed me aside to give Shane a birthday kiss.

"Your mom said no presents, but I just have to give you something," she said seductively, brushing her cocoa-glossed, nonsmear lips against his. She tried to wrap her arms around him, but he gently disengaged himself, glancing around the room with an air of utter bewilderment. (Think Owen Wilson in *Starsky and Hutch*.) If Shane was acting, he deserved top honors at the Golden Globe awards. With his widened eyes and look of jaw-dropping astonishment, he'd certainly nailed the part of Surprised Birthday Boy.

"Hey, this is great, you really got me," he said. "Mom, did you set this all up?" he called to a smiling blond woman standing at the edge of the crowd. She nodded and blew him a kiss.

"Man, I can't believe this," he blurted out, as the next wave of tanning-bed-basted, giggling starlets attacked him with wet kisses. "Hey, Jessie," he yelled, as they dragged him into the living room, "were you in on this?" He shot me a look that somehow managed to be calculating and sincere at the same time. Was this all an act? Who knew? Nothing was black-and-white in Hollywood, not even box office grosses.

I gave what I hoped was a small, sphinxlike grin. *"Moi?"* I asked innocently. "How would I know anything about the best-kept secret in Hollywood?"

A FEW MINUTES LATER, TRACY AND ELLIE ARRIVED. ELLIE IMMEDI-ately struck up a conversation with Lily Rockett, and Tracy edged over to where I was binging on standard Hollywood party fare—goat cheese and apricots coated in walnuts, caviar and salmon on water crackers, mini asparagus quiches, and brandied mango slices. *No cheese puffs or pigs in blankets here*, I thought.

"Are you okay?" Tracy asked, flashing on me scarfing down hors d'oeuvres like I hadn't eaten in weeks, a sure sign that I was stress eating from nerves. "Where's Shane?"

"Hah! He's missing in action." I grabbed a soda from a passing waiter. "And no, I'm not okay. This outfit was a huge mistake!" I gave a vicious tug to the edge of the peasant blouse that was threatening to crawl out of the elastic waistband of the Mexican "carnival" skirt.

"I thought you liked the look in the store," Tracy said sympathetically.

"I did, or at least I thought I did. But now I feel like a pathetic contestant on *What Not to Wear*. It's bad enough to be a fashion disaster, but what a place to do it! In case you haven't noticed," I said with heavy sarcasm, "we're surrounded by su-permodels and movie stars."

I did a double take as the host of a popular reality show walked by with his arm around a beautiful blonde wearing the "naughty schoolgirl look" that Britney had popularized in her "Hit Me Baby One More Time" video. She was wearing a private-school blazer with a crisp white blouse slashed open to the waist, a micromini pleated skirt, knee-high stockings, and Mary Janes. Surprisingly, it all worked, but I wondered why she was with someone old enough to be her father.

I edged closer to a giant palm tree, wishing I could just dis-appear into its green fronds, far away from the beautiful girls with their size zero figures and overbleached, Chiclet teeth. Where was Shane? He had vanished from the scene, appar-ently sucked into a vortex of Hollywood babes with bee-stung lips and necklines down to their navels.

"Why do you say you're a fashion disaster?" Tracy asked, yanking me back to the moment. "I think you look fine," she added in a trying-too-hard kind of way. Tracy, by the way, has absolutely no fashion sense and lives in a baggy white T-shirt and khaki pants, all year round.

"I look fine for a job in a mariachi band," I hissed. "If I had my guitar, I could stroll around, playing 'The Girl from Ipanema.'"

"Oh." She started to say something, thought better of it, and reached for a cheese canapé as she checked out the crowd.

I paused to guzzle my diet drink, as Charlize and Drew walked in hand in hand, followed by Scarlett and Cameron. Girls arriving at parties hand in hand was the new Hollywood trend and had been written up in *InStyle.* One theory was that Paris and Nicky Hilton had started the gimmick by strolling down the fashion show catwalks with their hands linked. Or maybe it was just a show of solidarity, pretty girls holding onto each other as they braved the bright lights and popping flashbulbs at Hollywood galas.

"At least there aren't any photographers here," I said, grateful that I wouldn't see a picture of myself decked out like I worked the dinner shift at Chi-Chi's.

"No, but there's paparazzi waiting at the bottom of the hill," Tracy said a little breathlessly. "We got in just before the onslaught. Somehow word's gotten out about the party. Lily Rockett set up a checkpoint with security, and you have to use valet parking now that the party's underway. She's determined to keep out photographers and gate-crashers." She stared at the crowd, trying to pick out celebrities. "So where's Shane?"

I gave a bitter little laugh. "Your guess is as good as mine. He's probably still getting kisses and birthday wishes from the girls." I was disappointed that Shane had left me stranded at his party and I felt a little flicker of annoyance curling in my chest. It was one thing to have to share him with his fans, but couldn't he even check back once in a while to see if I was enjoying myself? I was supposed to be his date!

"There you are," Lily Rockett said, appearing at my side,

giving me a little hug and suffocating me in a cloud of Chanel No. 19. "I've been looking all over for you, Jessie. I wanted to thank you for getting Shane here tonight. I can't believe we pulled it off." She clapped her hands delightedly and grabbed a peach cosmopolitan, as excited as if she had just cracked the DaVinci Code. "Where is he, anyway?" she said, scanning the crowd.

Tracy and I exchanged a look. *Maybe he's died and gone to supermodel heaven.* But the words died in my throat. It wasn't Lily Rockett's fault that Shane was on a major ego trip and had let himself be swallowed up by a tsunami of America's Top Models.

What I really said was, "I think he got swept away by the crowd, Mrs. Rockett. The last time I saw him, he was practically being carried out the sliding doors over there." I gestured to a wall of floor-to-ceiling glass panes that opened onto a flagstone patio, complete with Jacuzzi, surrounded by palm trees and a monster barbecue that looked big enough to roast an ox. There were colored lights at the base of the palms, sending jets of electric blue and hot pink into the night sky, while dozens of tiny white lights twinkled in the dense privacy hedge.

The music had changed to a hip-hop party mix, and I could see people dancing on the patio while the waiters served lime-green margaritas from a gurgling fountain. I started to head out there, ready to face the worst, when Lily grabbed me, linking her arm in mine. "Before I forget, Jessie, dear, I want you to meet someone." She linked arms with a portly, middle-aged man, pulling him into the circle with us. He had a bald head, a shiny face, and a tiny white goatee, which made him look like a slightly hairy hard-boiled egg. "Jessie Phillips, this is Edgar Harrison, the publisher of *Juicy*."

"*Juicy?*" I said blankly.

"The hottest new entertainment magazine in town, isn't it, Edgar, dear?" She smiled warmly at him and Edgar the Incredible Egg leaned in to her, basking in her attention. "They're doing a big feature on me in their first edition," she explained. "Hollywood Moms. It's hitting the stands next month. I think it will give my career a tremendous boost, and Shane just loves the pictures. The photographer you sent for the shoot was a genius, Edgar, a sheer genius. A true artist with a great sense of form and color. Those were the best pictures I've ever had taken. I'd like to hire him to do some new headshots for me."

"I'm sure that can be arranged. His job was very easy, because you could never take a bad picture, Lily." He turned and offered me a limp, sweaty palm, never taking his eyes off our hostess. I noticed he had snaked his arm around her waist and was looking at her with an expression of delirious devotion, like a pet cocker spaniel waiting for a meaty chew treat.

I was trying to think of a way to join Tracy, who'd drifted off to the buffet table, when Lily surprised me by saying, "You know, I think the two of you should get to know each other." She took each of us by the hand as if she was going to join us in some weird commitment ceremony, and I froze, nearly choking on my yogurt-covered soy nut. "I think fate brought you two together tonight," she said playfully. Edgar looked startled at the idea of cosmic intervention linking him with me, but Lily plunged ahead anyway.

"Really." His voice didn't go up or down, and his expression changed to one of beady suspicion as he took in my outfit for the first time.

"Oh yes," Lily babbled on in her girlish voice. "I think you two have a lot to offer each other. Jessie's visiting from out of town, Edgar, and I bet she has a completely different take on the whole Hollywood scene than"—she waved her hand vaguely toward the guests—"than most of the girls you find out here." She twirled a strand of honey-blond hair around her index finger. "It would be nice for the two of you to chat. Who knows? You might get some interesting story ideas for *Juicy*, and I know you want to appeal to the teen market as part of your demographics."

I looked around desperately for an avenue of escape, but Lily moved in front of me, blocking my path. "Edgar has wonderful commercial instincts, Jessie," she said, cocking an eyebrow at him. "I'm seeing exciting possibilities here."

Commercial instincts? Exciting possibilities? What's she talking about? I wondered. With that, she drifted away, leaving me face-to-face with Edgar, his fingers tapping nervously on his glass, his pale eyes flickering over me like a lizard.

"You're not from here?" He stared at me coolly, as if I were a side dish he hadn't ordered.

"I'm from Bedford, Connecticut," I said, wondering how I could make my escape. "The East Coast," I added, as if he needed a geography lesson.

"Hmmm," he said thoughtfully. "Connecticut. Not a flyover state, but still, I suppose it might work. I was really hoping for someone from the Midwest." He licked his lips and his voice trailed off uncertainly.

I knew that people in Hollywood considered everything between New York and L.A. to be "flyover" states, meaning places you fly over to get to somewhere else. Nowhere states, filled with uninteresting people who ate Velveeta cheese, belonged to bowling leagues, and probably watched *7th Heaven*.

"And you're a teenager." He said the words slowly, stretching out the syllables, and there was something reptilian about his unblinking gaze. He was still staring at me as though I were an alien life form. A not-too-bright alien life form.

"Yes, I am." I was starting to feel a little uncomfortable, waiting for him to ask me if I was from the future.

"Ah-ha. A teenager from Connecticut. That could be interesting." His fingernails began to beat a staccato on his glass, and I noticed they were buffed to a dull gloss with a French manicure. "Are you into raw foods, by any chance?"

"Raw foods? No, I'm afraid not. Should I be?"

He sighed. "We're thinking of doing a feature on it, and I'm having trouble finding someone who's actually managed to stick with it. I mean, how many radishes and garbanzo beans can a person eat, and live to tell about it?" He gave a grating cackle at his own wit. "It seems a lot of young actresses are into it; it seems to be very hot right now. Carol Alt has even written a book on it. I could interview her, of course." He scratched his tiny goatee. "But I'd rather do a Q & A with someone who Middle America could relate to—a real person, I mean."

By real person, I knew he meant a "civilian," someone not in show business. *Someone like me? Is this what Lily was getting at?* I suddenly realized that I had never told Shane I'd be leaving tomorrow. And Q & A meant "question and answer." If I didn't ditch Egg Man soon, I'd blow my last few hours with Shane, I thought, feeling a rumble of panic stir in my stomach as another Hollywood babe strolled by. She looked a little like Sarah Jessica Parker, and she fake-smiled at Edgar, probably thinking he was a film producer.

"I don't suppose you'd like to try the diet for a month or so, and keep a diary, would you?" Edgar's grating voice dragged me back into the conversation. "You could make notes every day, something clever, like a teenage version of *Bridget Jones.*" His pale face became animated as he warmed to the topic. "We'd run it as a monthly feature, and of course, you would get your own byline. We might even expand it into recipes and raw-food restaurant reviews. I think they have a couple of places down in Venice or Hermosa Beach that serve strictly raw foods."

I shook my head. "No, I don't think so. As far as I know, some raw-food diets include meat." I said helpfully. "So that wouldn't work for me, because I never eat meat."

Why didn't I just tell him that I didn't live out here, and I wouldn't be around to check out those restaurants, anyway? I craned my neck, trying to get a glimpse of a blond hunk at the edge of the living room, inching toward the kitchen. Shane? My heart thudded until he turned and I realized it was just another good-looking guy.

Edgar was still studying me thoughtfully. "Ah, you're one of those vegans," he said. "That's very hot right now. An interesting trend."

"No, I'm not a vegan, I'm a vegetarian." My eyes darted toward the patio as a crowd surged back inside. Was Shane still out there? I hated the idea of trailing after him like a lovesick puppy dog, but what else could I do? What if I didn't see him again until the party was over?

He chuckled dryly. "You'll have to enlighten me. What is the difference between a vegetarian and a vegan?"

"Vegetarians don't eat meat, but they do eat eggs and milk and cheese," I said, still peering over his shoulder. "Vegans don't eat eggs or any dairy products. So, the easy way to remember it is that vegetarians eat nothing with a face, and vegans eat nothing with a mother." I had been asked this so many times, I had a pat answer. I was giving him the *Dummies* version, of course. There are ovo vegetarians and ovo-lacto vegetarians, but I didn't think he wanted to get into all that. And I certainly didn't either. I looked around for Tracy, planning my escape.

He smiled. "An interesting distinction. You're an entertaining girl, Jessie Phillips. I'll just make a note of that." He gave me a sharp, speculative look before pulling out a tiny leather note-book and scribbling for a moment with a gold pen. "Would you mind if I asked you a few questions?" Without waiting for an answer, he whipped out an index card and slipped on a pair of wire-rimmed glasses that made him look vaguely like Benjamin Franklin.

"Well, I was just going to get a refill . . ." I began, as he grabbed a glass from a passing waiter and took a sniff before thrusting it at me. "A virgin piña colada, delicious. Drink this while we talk, my dear. I'll just take a few minutes of your time."

"Okay." I shifted uneasily from one foot to the other, trying to force down an image of Shane lounging in the hot tub out-side, surrounded by Beyonce look-alikes. I took a sip of the pastel-colored drink. It tasted like cotton candy.

"I'll say a word or phrase, and you tell me whatever comes to mind." He frowned when I hesitated. "Just pretend it's a game, and don't think too hard. Say the first thing that comes into your head."

"Got it." I took a deep breath, trying to force some enthusi-asm into my voice. How was I going to get rid of this guy?

"The O.C."

"The O.C. Love it. Definitely one of my favorite shows," I said in a clipped voice. Something was wrong because Edgar scowled, making an irritated noise deep in his throat, like a cat about to hack up a hairball. He peered at me over his glasses, making a speeding-up motion with his hand, those glassy, trout eyes fixed on me.

"Oh, you want me to keep on going?" I improvised quickly, wanting to get this over with, so I could track down my Shane. "Okay, well, let me see. Well, I love the characters, love the dialogue. Ben McKenzie and Adam Brody are awesome. And of course Rachel Bilson and Mischa Barton are amazing actresses and very different from each other. I think that's what makes the show so exciting, the contrast between the characters. You never know what's going to happen from week to week."

"Good point." He nodded approvingly. "Anything else?"

"When I watched the show back in Bedford I thought the actresses playing the girls at Beverly Hills High were over the top. They seemed so impossibly thin and gorgeous; everyone's a size zero with good hair." I paused, thinking. "But after I came out here I realized that California girls really do look like that. Everyone back at Fairmont Academy loves Mischa Barton in her ballet flats and her cute little shrugs." I laughed. "Come to think of it, they all want to look like Mischa and they all want to date Ben McKenzie."

For the next twenty minutes, Edgar peppered me with questions about what's "in" and what's "out." (Inquiring teens want to know!) Here is a short list: hair extensions (Can be "in" or "out," but if you have fabulous hair like Jennifer Aniston's, do you really need them?), Paris Hilton (In. Too overexposed, but love her look), *I Married a Princess* (Out. Boring. Should be called *I Married a Guy with the Same Name as the Friendly Ghost*), Britney and Kevin (Who cares?), Ashlee

Simpson (In, but hope she's not still lip-synching), spray tans (In. A cool way to look tan even if you feel like you're in a car wash), and fur coats (Out. Would you wear your cat?). I was surprised that Edgar listened carefully and wrote down my answers as if my opinions really mattered.

I was just about to edge away when Shane appeared at my side, slipping his arm around my waist. "Hi, darlin'," he said, as if he hadn't left me stranded for nearly a half hour. He leaned over to nuzzle my cheek for a split second and spotted Edgar. "Sorry about the disappearing act, Jessie, but I see you're in good hands. Hey, Edgar, how ya doin'?"

"Good evening, Shane." Edgar puffed out his chest in a self-important way and I stifled a giggle. The man was so pretentious! All I could think of was how desperately I wanted to be rid of him and be alone with Shane. "I think I've found my girl," Edgar said, nodding his head toward me.

Shane laughed. "Yeah? Well, I saw her first, pal," he joked, squeezing my waist. "She's my date tonight."

Edgar colored, his tiny goatee quivering in indignation. "I'm talking about an employment opportunity," he said quickly. "Your mother knew I was looking for a teen columnist for *Juicy* and she insisted Jessie would be perfect. At first I had my doubts," he said, gulping his frozen drink, "but now I see that Lily's judgment was excellent as usual. Jessie is not only up on the latest trends, but she has a unique take on them and a colorful way of expressing herself. Lily was right."

"Is someone talking about me?" Lily was pushing past us to the kitchen, but she stopped to rest her hand on Edgar's arm. "I hope it's all good."

Edgar lifted her hand to his lips and kissed it. "Lily, my dear, thanks to you, I've found my teen columnist. It's a summer internship, but we can probably stretch it into something else if it really takes off."

A summer internship on a Hollywood magazine? Was he serious? My mind skidded to a halt and I felt my insides freeze as Lily leaned over and enveloped me in an excited hug. I glanced over Lily's shoulder, trying to size up the situation. Edgar certainly looked serious, his icy green eyes flickering as he raised his banana daiquiri in a toast. "To the new star of *Juicy*," he said solemnly. I felt a sickly smile spread over my face and my mouth went dry as our eyes locked. *Why hadn't I spoken up when I had the chance?*

"Well, Edgar, I hate to say I told you so, but I told you so," Lily said with a giggle. "She's perfect, isn't she?" She drew back to look at me. "Your mother's going to be so proud of you, Jessie. Just think, you just flew out here and you've already nabbed one of the hottest jobs in town!"

I felt light-headed, and I swayed slightly as a loud, rushing sound pulsed through my ears. Was I having an out-of-body experience? Surprise, excitement, and fear swirled through me, like colors in a toy kaleidoscope.

Shane looked at me, his dark eyes snapping with fire. He seemed jazzed by the sudden turn of events, not even aware that I was in danger of passing out cold! "So it's true? You're really stayin' out here for the summer? And workin' for *Juicy*? Jess, that is so awesome!"

I hesitated, trying to find the right words to turn down the most exciting opportunity of my entire life. There was no way I could even consider taking Edgar up on his offer; it was out of the question. I was leaving for Bedford the very next day. I had no place to stay in Hollywood, and besides, I knew my mother would have a fit if I even suggested it.

The whole idea was crazy, impossible, and I knew I had to say no. And I had to say it right this second, because everyone was staring at me, waiting for my answer.

I looked straight at Shane, mesmerized by those sexy dark eyes. And then, without even meaning to, I said the words that set everything in motion, the words that changed the course of my life and set me on the Hollywood fast track.

"You're right, Shane," I told him. "It is totally awesome!"

Chapter Five

★

"SO IT HAPPENED JUST LIKE THAT?" IT WAS AFTER MIDNIGHT, AND Tracy and I were sitting on Ellie's balcony, splitting a pint of Chunky Monkey with the soft sounds of Norah Jones drifting over us from the boom box in the living room. "Lily recommended you to this Edgar guy, and he interviewed you on the spot?" Tracy propped her feet up on the wrought-iron balcony and pulled one of Ellie's pastel pashminas tightly around her shoulders. It was a beautiful star-studded night with a cool, salty breeze rolling in from the ocean. "You must have really impressed him, Jess," she said admiringly. "I would have been completely tongue-tied, I don't know how you did it. People would kill for that job."

"I didn't even know it was an interview," I said, staring out at the flickering lights on the Santa Monica Pier, "so maybe that helped. All I had to do was say the first thing that popped into my head. I had no idea how much was riding on my answers." I shook my head, surprised that Edgar Harrison thought I had my finger on the pulse of teenagers all over the country.

I was preoccupied, my mind racing through what I should do next. Besides the *Juicy* offer, there was the whole Shane issue to figure out, but the magic of the evening was making my brain a little hazy. How would our relationship would play itself out? Or did we even have a relationship? I felt a flash of uncertainty fly through my gut.

I had spent only a few minutes with Shane at the party and he'd given me a chaste kiss on the cheek when I said my good-byes and left with Ellie and Tracy. He'd seemed pleased that Edgar had offered me the position at *Juicy*, but was he being sincere? I remembered the bevy of Hollywood babes surrounding him from the moment he walked in the door. Was it realistic to think he was going to spend every spare minute with me if I moved to Hollywood for the summer? He was probably dating someone, wasn't he? I was surprised that Heidi Hopkins wasn't at the party, but someone said she was doing a photo shoot in Paris. I wondered if she was on the guest list, and even more important, I wondered if Shane was still seeing her. She had been the reason I didn't even say good-bye to Shane after the *Reckless Summer* shoot, and I felt a bitter taste in my mouth whenever I thought of the blond-haired beauty.

I was so lost in thought, I didn't hear Ellie slip onto the balcony, dressed in a white terry robe and slippers. She was sipping a chai latte from a Garfield mug, and her liquid eyes were glowing, her hair loose around her shoulders.

"Didn't you hear the phone? That was Lily who just called." She sat down next to us, her smile flashing excitement. "Tracy, Edgar wants you to work for *Juicy*, too. There's a spot open in their photography department. Lily told him you'd done a video diary of *Reckless Summer* and he agreed it would be right up your alley."

Tracy swallowed hard and took her feet off the railing. "Really? He's offering me a summer job, without even talking to me?" Her face lit up with excitement and she shivered a little in the night air. "I can't believe it, can you, Jess? I was planning on going home tomorrow."

Ellie laughed. "You see how perfectly it's all working out. Jessie will have her own column, you'll have a photography internship, Tracy, and I'll have company for the summer. You'll both stay here with me, of course."

"We couldn't," I began, glancing at Tracy. It was one thing to stay for the weekend, but could we really impose on Ellie for the whole summer? And I reminded myself that I still hadn't cleared anything with my mother, and that she was expecting me back in Bedford tomorrow evening.

"Don't be silly. Of course you can, I've got tons of room. I don't want to hear another word about it. It's a done deal." Ellie stifled a yawn and stood up. "I'm afraid I've got to get to bed,

I've got a big show next week. Jessie, we'll talk to your mother in the morning and straighten everything out." She must have seen my hesitant expression because she added, "Don't worry, I can be very persuasive. And Tracy, I'll talk to your mother, too. I think we should make the calls early, to allow for the three-hour time difference." I nodded, wondering how my mother would react when she heard I'd accepted a summer job in Hollywood.

"Night, girls," she said, vanishing inside.

Tracy looked stunned. "This is unbelievable," she said slowly. "I've got a photography internship with a hot new magazine. I guess I'll be taking pictures of celebrities, going to big events and film premieres." Her voice sounded a little flat and I wondered if she felt nervous at suddenly being offered such a high-profile job. Tracy is really talented but has been known to get butterflies when she's thrown into new situations, and this was far beyond what either one of us had ever imagined.

"But you're happy about it, right, Trace?"

She gave a nervous laugh and then smiled, as if someone had turned on a switch inside her. "I'm beyond happy, I'm just fighting off a major anxiety attack. This will be dynamite on my résumé, but do you think my mother will go for it? She doesn't even know Ellie."

"No, but she knows my mother. And Ellie has been my mom's friend for years and years. Honestly, Tracy, if you want the job, it's yours. You heard what Ellie said. She's happy to have us stay here."

"I heard it," Tracy said slowly, a slow smile spreading over her face. "I just can't believe it."

Things moved so quickly, I barely had time to think about Shane and was surprised when he called in midafternoon. I had spent most of the morning on the phone with my mom, working out the details of my stay and telling her what clothes I'd like her to ship out to me. She had a long talk with Ellie, and to my amazement had agreed to let me spend the summer with her. Tracy's mom had been a harder sell, but in the end, it all worked out, just like Ellie had predicted.

"How's my favorite columnist?" Shane's sexy voice raced over the wire and I sank down on the edge of the bed, curling my feet under me.

"I think I'm still in shock," I said slowly. "I still can't believe it's really happening."

Shane chuckled. "Well, get used to it, darlin', because now you've made the big time. I can see it now, your face on the cover of *People* magazine: Hollywood's new teen star."

"No danger of that," I said. "Writers never get on the cover, and I'll never be a star anyway, because my acting days are over. I'm very happy sticking to journalism. I still can't believe I landed the job."

"Well, whatever you did, you must have knocked the socks off ole Edgar. He's still talking about you."

"Really? I was just being myself. It was all because of your birthday party, you know. If I hadn't met Edgar last night, and if your mom hadn't recommended me to him, none of this would have happened." I paused. "Instead of being on the staff of *Juicy*, I'd be on my way back to Bedford. I'm a small-town girl, Shane, things like this just don't happen to me."

Shane laughed. "Oh, I don't know about that, Jess. Remember what I told you about Hollywood? Anything can happen at any time and your wildest dreams can come true. I had a feeling you'd be out here for the summer, and I knew for sure we'd be spendin' lots of time together."

"You did?"

"I sure did, darlin'. In fact, now that you've got the *Juicy* job, I reckon we'll be together every single minute."

Really? Every single minute? I flashed back to the party scene, when Shane was engulfed by girls who looked like they had just stepped out of a Victoria's Secret catalog. And come to think of it, he hadn't put up much resistance! "I think you'll be pretty busy yourself this summer," I said wryly. "You know, you never told me what happened at that meeting with your agent at the Ivy the other night. Is that movie deal off, or on?"

"Oh, nothing's definite yet," he said easily. "One of those back-burner projects. You know what we always say in Texas: you gotta drop a lot of lines in the water if you're hopin' for a fish to bite. You won't get anywhere just sittin' on the dock."

I laughed. "I'll have to remember that." Shane had a collection of down-home expressions that he sprinkled into the conversation and I wondered if this was part of the "sexy cowboy" persona he created, just like the Stetson hat and the tooled leather boots. He had once told me, "It's not who you are that counts in Hollywood, Jessie. It's who people think you are."

"But the real reason I called, Jess, is to make sure you kept tonight open, so we can celebrate together. I'm planning on taking you someplace really special." He must have sensed my hesitation because he rushed on. "I won't take no for an answer, Jess. You promised me I could take you out in style, and that's exactly what I'm going to do."

"So you're making me an offer I can't refuse," I said jokingly. "Okay, I'll bite. Just tell me what time you'll pick me up." Moments later, I asked Ellie if we could make a quick trip back to Melrose Avenue. It was my big night on the town with Shane, and this time I was determined to wear something fabulous!

"WOW, YOU LOOK BEAUTIFUL!" SHANE HELD OPEN THE DOOR OF his silver Jag and let out a long, appreciative whistle as I stepped inside. Thanks to Ellie, I had bought a drop-dead-gorgeous filmy dress, a delicate green-and-white print that showed off my legs and flowed when I moved. It was the most spectacular outfit I had ever owned, and Ellie had loaned me a pair of strappy high heels to go with it.

"Thanks," I said, suddenly feeling a little shy, and trying not to wobble on the three-inch heels. Shane looked amazing in a gray, tailored suit with a crisp white shirt. I realized it was the first time I had seen him dressed formally, and I felt my breath catch in my throat, he was so gorgeous! He pulled on his Ray-Bans as he headed up the Pacific Coast Highway and slid a Jack Johnson CD in the tape deck.

It was a beautiful, soft evening, and I leaned my head back, letting the cool ocean breeze drift over my face. "Where are we heading?" I asked, surprised that he didn't take the Interstate 10 exit for downtown L.A., but instead headed up the San Diego Freeway into the Malibu Hills. The hills were awesome and I craned my neck to gawk at mansions the size of hotels nestled along the ridge, nearly hidden by masses of towering trees.

"The Getty Center is the first stop," Shane said.

"Oh, that's the place Tracy's always wanted to see—" I started to say, but Shane cut in swiftly.

"We'll take her with us next time, but tonight is just for the two of us. I haven't had a chance to really welcome you to town, Jessie. Or to spend much time alone with you." He flashed a rueful smile.

"You can make it up to me," I suggested teasingly.

"Oh, I plan to," he promised. "I've got lots of surprises for you tonight, but we're starting with the best view of Los Angeles you'll ever find. And it's at the Getty." We suddenly turned off Interstate 405 onto a narrow side road, drove for a few miles, and pulled into the Getty parking lot. "Best of all," Shane added, "no one ever expects to see me at an art museum, so I don't get hassled here. Sometimes people do a double take, but then they decide that it can't possibly be me."

"I never thought of you as the art museum type," I admitted.

"It's all because of my mom," he said seriously. "She had art books lying around the house all the time when I was growing up and she was always taking me to museums and galleries. I think if she hadn't gone into acting, she would have been a painter." We stepped into the tram to take us up to the museum and Shane continued, "I come here every chance I get. They have new exhibits all the time and there's a photography one coming up that I know Tracy will like. I'll check the date before we leave tonight."

"She'd like that." So Shane was an art lover? As usual, he was full of surprises.

We spent an hour or so looking at an exhibit of European paintings, including an amazing Cezanne still-life watercolor, and then headed up to the observation deck for the "360-degree view" of Los Angeles Shane had promised me.

It was awesome, and we stood silently watching as the San Gabriel Mountains turned a dusky lavender color as the sun dropped in the sky. Beneath us were the checkerboard streets of Los Angeles, stretching out to the hazy Santa Monica Mountains in the distance. If I turned around, I could see the sparkling Pacific in the distance, crystalline blue, shimmering out to the horizon. Shane was right, each view was spectacular; I could see why he loved it here.

"Do you like it?" Shane said softly. He was standing very close and as he dipped his head to brush my cheek with his lips, my heart did a funny little lurch. He surprised me by lifting my hand and gently kissing the tips of my fingers and then the center of my palm.

"Do I like it?" I repeated stupidly. His lips on my fingertips had thrown me into a state of temporary insanity, and now I could feel my heart hammering in my chest. I leaned into his chest, with his arms around my waist, and he held me close. I could have stood there for a very long time, maybe until dawn. I swear the earth stood still.

"Yes," I blurted out. "I like it very much. In fact, it's the most amazing place I've ever seen," I told him. "I'm glad you brought me here." *So much for playing it cool!* I thought wryly. The Getty was amazing but *True Confessions* time: Shane could have taken me to a tractor pull and I would have felt that same silly buzz deep inside me! That's how exciting it was to be with him.

"I knew you'd like it," he said with a satisfied grin. "I wanted you to see it, because it's special to me. I've been up here dozens of times, and I get knocked out by the view every single time. Sometimes when I've got a problem, I come here to clear my head. I can't explain it, but there's just something about this place. I can stand here with the sun on my face, staring at the mountains, and whatever was botherin' me seems to disappear."

I nodded. "I know what you mean. I feel the same way when I walk along the ocean. I watch the waves rolling in, and the sand scrunching up between my toes, and somehow whatever was bothering me doesn't seem so important."

I looked around the deck and realized no one had recognized Shane. Maybe it was the tailored suit, so different from his usual jeans and cowboy boots, or maybe it was what he had said: that no one thought of the Sexiest Teen Star in America hanging out at a museum.

"I like it when you're incognito," I said, snuggling against him. "No delirious fans, no one shoving a piece of paper in your face for an autograph."

"And no paparazzi. That's why I picked this place." He glanced around the deck and seemed relieved to see that no one was paying the slightest bit of attention to him. He looked at his watch. "Getting hungry?"

"A little, but I don't want to leave," I said. "I'm enjoying this too much." There was a golden glow over the beautiful travertine marble buildings, and the whole scene was bathed in a honeyed warmth.

"We don't have to leave. We can eat right here." He flashed his trademark smile. "I always try to think ahead, Jess, and I ordered a picnic lunch for us. I even got you the Mediterranean Vegetable Baguette." He pulled an index card out of his jacket pocket and reeled off the ingredients. "How does this sound? Roasted red pepper, eggplant, fennel with wilted spinach, and olive tapenade." He looked at me searchingly. "That's okay, isn't it? I know you're a vegetarian."

I was floored. "This was really thoughtful of you, Shane."

"Oh, wait, there's more," he said, still reading. "We're starting with lemon dill hummus and pita chips. And I ordered roasted vegetable cream cheese with crostini."

He looked so earnest that my heart melted, and I kissed him

on the cheek. "Shane, you always surprise me. This is the nicest thing you could have done for me." The idea of Shane going to all that trouble to order a vegetarian meal really touched me, especially since I knew his favorite meal was Texas barbecue with big helpings of red-hot chili.

"Well, I thought it would be good for the two of us to eat without being interrupted, and without people gawking. I know you were disappointed at the party my mom threw for me last night. I don't think we said more than a few sentences to each other." He smiled. "Of course, you did get to meet Edgar, so it wasn't a complete waste."

"It definitely wasn't a waste. Just think, I'm spending the summer in Hollywood, and it's all because of Edgar."

We picked up the picnic lunch and headed to the South Pavilion Terrace. Shane was right. No one was giving him a second glance and I was excited at the thought of having him all to myself for the evening. I noticed he chose to sit with his back facing the other diners, just like he had done at the café in Venice Beach. He took a quick glance around before removing his shades and laying them on the table.

"You have it down to a science," I said, as he poured us each a glass of mineral water. "Was it always like this? Having to plan where you go, and learning how not to be spotted?"

He nodded. "Everything changed once I did those first two movies for New Line." I remembered Shane starring in a couple of action-adventure films that were supposed to take place in eastern Europe, but actually were shot on a studio backlot in

Century City. "Before that, I couldn't get myself arrested. But once the first movie was released it really hit big, and the sequel was even bigger. They timed it just right; it was a summer movie and the schools had just gotten out. Anyway, the box office grosses were good, and before you know it, New Line had really pumped up the media hype, and I was doing back-to-back interviews with *E.T.*, *Access Hollywood*, and just about every other show you can think of."

"Sounds exciting." I sampled the pita dip, thinking that Shane was so casual about a world that most people could only dream about.

He grimaced. "It's not as much fun as you think. You sit in a hotel suite, and entertainment reporters line up in the hotel corridor, waiting their turn. They each have fifteen minutes to interview you, but they all ask the same questions, so you find yourself answering the same questions over and over. There's no end to it. Smile, smile some more, give the little spiel you memorized, and make it sound fresh and new each time. Then stand up, shake hands, pose for a picture, and bingo, another reporter sits down. In a way, it's one of the hardest acting jobs in the world. It looks like you could just phone it in, but believe me, it's tough. At least if you do it right."

"Can't you just be yourself?" I loved hearing Shane talk about show business, and it made me realize he didn't have the picture-perfect life his fans imagined.

"Not really." Shane shook his head. "You've got to be a superstar and a regular guy at the same time. My mom told me to always have three or four stories to tell, and if you can, try to tell a few jokes on yourself. That's the same advice they give you when you go on the *Tonight Show*. Have a few funny stories and make sure you get them in the conversation. Don't try to improvise; know those stories and have them down pat. And of course, make sure they're just as funny as you can make them. Keep 'em short with a great punchline."

"I thought all that stuff was spontaneous."

"It looks that way, but it's not, really. You sit down with one of the show's producers, and she asks you for your three or four 'stories' ahead of time. You actually tell them to her, and she decides which ones are the best and passes that information along to the host. That way, he'll steer the conversation in that direction, so you get a chance to tell them."

"So he sort of sets up the story?"

Shane nodded. "That's right. If one of your stories is about wiping out on a surfboard, he'll say something about you living on the ocean or about your being athletic. Or if something funny happened in eastern Europe on the set of your last movie, he'll ask what it was like shooting in Yugoslavia. Then that's your cue to jump in with a funny story about eating beet soup for breakfast or wearing three layers of underwear when you're sleeping in a room with icicles on the dresser. It gets a big laugh and everybody's happy. After all, if you look good, the host looks good."

"Wow, it sounds like you've got to be thinking every minute."

"Yeah, they don't want any dead air, and the time really whizzes by. You've got only seven minutes to promote your new movie, and you want the audience to fall in love with you and rush out and see it. You can mention the name of your movie once or twice, but they get ticked off if you repeat it over and over." He paused. "In fact, that's a good way not to get invited back. I did that a couple of times when I started out, but I learned my lesson the hard way," he said ruefully. "The publicist really tore into me after the show, even though it was her fault. Nobody warned me, and I was young and clueless."

"Shane, you could never be clueless! I've seen you doing interviews and you look relaxed, like you're really enjoying it."

"Well, that's the main thing, to look like you're having fun. And my mom always reminds me to act like a nice guy, and not come across like I'm on some ego trip."

"But you *are* a nice guy!" I teased him. "The *Enquirer* said you were funny, smart, one of the nicest guys in Hollywood."

"That's what they say this week!" Shane said feelingly. "Next week, it could be completely different. The press can turn on you in an instant, and believe me, I've felt their sting." I remembered that he'd gone through some bad press with the tabloids during the *Reckless Summer* shoot, and they'd portrayed him as a Hollywood playboy, hanging out till dawn on Sunset Strip.

"The whole publicity thing sounds a lot tougher than I thought."

"It comes with the territory. The problem kicks in after the first twenty or thirty interviews," he said wryly. "Then it gets to be a real drag. I don't have a choice about it, anyway," he went on. "It's in my contract. I have to do so many hours and so many days of publicity each time a movie comes out. It's all part of the business."

"Shane, I'll be one of those pesky entertainment reporters once I start my *Juicy* job next week." I had a sudden thought: what if I was assigned to interview Shane? Or would that be a wild conflict of interest? Edgar seemed to be a big fan of Lily's, so it was unlikely that he'd want me to write anything about Shane that wasn't flattering.

He paused. "You know, for some reason, I sure talk about myself a lot when I'm with you, Jessie. You must be sick of listenin' to all this."

I shook my head. "I could never get sick of listening to you. I love hearing about your life." I leaned over to sample the roasted vegetable dip and crostini. "It's like having a guide to a whole world I don't know anything about. I'm on the outside looking in." It was true. I had had a brief fling with movie making when Fearless Productions had filmed a movie in my hometown a few weeks earlier, but the whole L.A. scene was beyond anything I had ever imagined. I felt like a country bumpkin, listening to Shane describing his wheeling and dealing with the Hollywood players.

"But I want to find out more about you." He looked at me with those startlingly beautiful eyes, dark and mysterious. "You're very different from the other girls I know, Jessie. I've never met anyone like you, and I've been wondering about something: what would you have done if you hadn't been offered the *Juicy* job? Would we have seen each other again? Would you have walked out of my life, just like that?"

That was a tough one. "I don't know," I said honestly. "I was all set to head home to Bedford until I met Edgar at the party. My mom had planned on my working at her antiques shop, and I guess I was going to have a quiet summer." I decided not to mention that I was supposed to visit Marc LaPierre in New Orleans. Marc was a great-looking guy I had met the previous summer, and we had an on-again, off-again relationship.

Marc was phenomenal—funny, drop-dead gorgeous—and there was a sizzling chemistry between us. He was thoughtful and considerate and had even surprised me by flying up from New Orleans to visit me in Bedford during the movie shoot. He'd suspected something was going on, and probably guessed I was attracted to Shane, but he refused to give up, and was counting on seeing me again in Louisiana. I still hadn't told him I'd be in L.A. for the summer, and knew I'd have to call him sometime and tell him about the change in plans.

Marc was still a wild card, and at some point in my life, I was going to have to decide what to do about that relationship. He was a great guy, and it wasn't fair to keep him guessing.

Tracy kept telling me that if Shane weren't in the picture, Marc would be Mr. Right, the kind of guy you would consider a "keeper." But facts were facts. Shane *was* in the picture, and one steamy look from him had the power to drive all other boys out of my memory banks!

Shane's sexy voice dragged me back to the present. "Well,

I'm lucky it worked out this way, Jess. I always want to be part of your life, you know. There's no way I'm givin' you up—you're stuck with me like white on rice, like we say down south."

He reached across the table to lock my fingers through his, his grip warm and thrilling. He threw in a toe-curling smile, just for good measure.

"White on rice?" I laughed at yet another of Shane's cornball sayings. He seemed to have an inexhaustible supply of them, but somehow they seemed right, not hokey, when he said them. "Sounds pretty permanent to me." My heart pinged oddly, and I reminded myself to be cautious. Hadn't I been taken in before? *Take it slow, Jess,* I said silently.

"It is permanent." He had a low, throaty voice that made him sound like he smoked, but he didn't. *Permanent? Was anything really permanent out here in the land of make-believe?* His warm and fuzzy words meant little in the real world of Hollywood, but I didn't feel like arguing the point.

"If you say so," I said softly. We locked eyes for a moment; just a look from him could make me go weak in the knees.

He laughed, breaking the tension. "I think we've seen enough art for one night," he said, cleaning up the remains of our picnic. "Let's go to the beach; there's nothing better than Malibu after dark."

Half an hour later, when were tooling down the Pacific Coast Highway, headed for a walk on the beach, Shane's cell rang, belting out "Freebird" from Lynyrd Skynyrd. "Gotta take it," Shane said apologetically, glancing at the number.

"Hey babe, what's up?" *Babe?* I immediately went on red alert, straining forward a little in the seat, wishing I could hear the other half of the conversation. "Now?" Shane looked over at me, his eyebrows raised, and then said smoothly, "Actually, I'm kind of busy, I'm on a date. Hey, this is Saturday night, date night, you know. Can't a guy get a little R & R?" He laughed to soften his words. "Hang on a sec."

He punched a button and glanced over at me. "Jess, do you mind if we scratch that walk on the beach till later? We'll still do it, but we just need to make a quick pit stop at a hot new club. It'll only take twenty minutes, honestly." When I hesitated, his voice was wheedling. "It's my publicist, Adriana. She sort of promised that I'd make a quick appearance and didn't bother to tell me. Honestly, we'll be in and out of there in a flash. I promise."

I sighed. Once again, plans for a quiet, intimate evening with Shane were shattered. "Sure, Shane," I told him, trying not to let the disappointment filter into my voice. "We'll hit the club first. Whatever you say."

Chapter Six

SHANE SEEMED TENSE AND PREOCCUPIED AS WE TOOK THE PCH straight back to Santa Monica, turning west off Wilshire, heading into the club district. We passed Sugar, Zanzibar, the Temple Bar and a string of other hot clubs, their dazzling neon lights shimmering in the late-night heat. The doors were flung wide open and the thumping hip-hop music poured out, hanging on the sultry air before drifting down the darkened street.

There was a soft breeze blowing in from the ocean and it felt wildly exciting to be in California with Shane. When he reached over and gave my knee a quick squeeze, I could feel a tingle in every part of my body. I glanced into a packed club called Fourteen Below as we stopped at a red light.

"Looks like a popular spot," I commented. I remembered

Ellie saying that this was a hot area for new bands to try out their songs and that some of the edgier groups had managed to get their work featured on the soundtrack for *The* O.C.

"Yeah, if you're gonna open a new club, this is as good a place as any. But it's a really competitive business and most of them don't last a year. By the time a club is hot, it's over and people have moved on to the next one. And some of the best places don't even have a sign on the door. You just have to know about them. By the time the tourists discover them, they're history."

Shane managed to snare a parking spot on a side street as a gunmetal Porsche Carrera pulled out, tires squealing. After turning off the ignition, he sat still for a few moments, staring tensely out the tinted windows, making no move to get out of the car.

"Shane, what's up? Is something wrong?" I started to feel a little nervous myself, picking up on an uneasy vibe from him. I stared out at the street, too, but couldn't imagine what had set him on red alert. A group of teens dressed for prom night strolled by, the girls self-conscious in their filmy dresses and stiletto heels, the guys looking uncomfortable in their tuxes. A young couple walked by hand in hand, did a double take when they spotted the silver Jag, and then ambled back for another look. They stared at the tinted windows for a few moments and then moved on, nuzzling each other, sharing some private joke. "Well, what is it?" I persisted, letting my breath out in a little puff. "You're making me nervous."

"I'm sorry, Jess. It's probably nothing." I could only see his profile in the darkened car, but from the tightness around his mouth and the determined set to his jaw, I knew something was up.

"It doesn't feel like nothing," I said gently.

"You know, Jess, I always trust my gut, and I just don't have a good feeling about tonight. I think I should have had Kevin order some security, that's all." He shook his head. "Adriana caught me off guard, and I just didn't think of it. And now here we are . . ." His voice trailed off uncertainly.

"But why in the world do we need security?" I was baffled, and couldn't imagine why he was so worried. No one had even recognized him or asked for an autograph for the past couple of hours, and I was sure our luck would continue.

"We've been lucky so far tonight, Jess. It doesn't look like there'll be any media here, but you never know."

I gave him a reassuring smile and reached over to touch his hand. "Shane, relax. Nobody knows you're going to be here tonight. We're just going to drop in for a quick appearance, that's all. You said yourself it's going to be a surprise."

"That's what Adriana told me. She said she wanted to surprise the owner, but I wouldn't put it past her to tip off the paparazzi."

"I hope not," I said feelingly. "Why would she do that?"

He gave a cynical half-laugh. "More buzz for the club and a nicer bonus for Adriana. I don't feel like dealing with these guys tonight, that's for sure."

I had seen the paparazzi in action once before, during an arson incident at the *Reckless Summer* shoot, and I understood Shane's concern.

"Blue Lotus, I've never even heard of the place," he muttered, glancing at the address he'd gotten from Adriana. "I wonder if it's some little hole in the wall."

"So it's not A-list?" I joked, trying out my Hollywood lingo.

He shook his head. "Afraid not. I still can't believe Adriana did this without asking me," he said tightly. "I bet she owes the club owner a favor, and she's paying him off by promising I'll drop in tonight."

"Is this the way they usually do things?"

"It's the way Adriana does things. You know the saying about robbing Peter to pay Paul? That's what she does all the time. She's one of the best publicists in the business, but she has a way of springing things on me out of nowhere. She knows her way around the media, though, and she's got some great contacts. She's gotten me some top-level interviews, and I really owe that *People* magazine cover to her." He sighed. "So I guess I can't complain, right? A lot of people would love to be in my shoes. My mom always reminds me of that."

"Will I be dealing with her? Or people like her?" I couldn't believe I started at *Juicy* next week. I was going to be an entertainment reporter! Not a star, of course, but definitely on the fringes of show business, maybe even a player, as Tracy would say.

"Yeah, I guess you will be, darlin'. Publicists will be fallin' all over you, trying to get a mention for their clients. Edgar will decide which offers to take, which artists to interview. He's out there competing with a new magazine, so he probably won't take any chances in the beginning. He'll want the usual selection of heavy hitters on the cover. Brad, Angelina, Jennifer, Lindsay, Mischa, Paris—they'll sell the magazine every time." He took the keys out of the ignition. "Show time," he said, sighing a little as he opened the car door.

MINUTES LATER, A BOUNCER WHO WAS A DEAD RINGER FOR VIN Diesel recognized Shane and gave him the high sign. He whispered something into his headset, then hopped athletically over the velvet rope, heading straight toward us. Dozens of people who were waiting in line stopped talking and pointed to Shane, nudging each other, exchanging excited looks. A surprise appearance by a major star was something they hadn't bargained on, and they started whipping out their cameras and cell phones.

A girl who looked about twelve and a half, wearing a pale rose Pokemon baby tee, jabbed me hard in the ribs. Her T-shirt was so tight, it looked like her chest was swathed in a bright pink Ace bandage. "Is that Shane Rockett? Is that really him? Wow, he is so hot!"

I ignored her, edging a little closer to Shane, who was watching the crowd, his eyes narrowed and his expression serious. When I touched his arm, he glanced at me and grabbed my hand, lacing his fingers through mine in a bone-crunching grip. Immediately my antennae shot up. *What had we gotten ourselves into?*

"I knew this would happen," he muttered, his voice tight. "Once we get inside, we'll be okay. I should have told Adriana we'd come in the back way. Man, this is a zoo." He drew his arm tightly around my waist and I could feel his heart thumping hard in his chest.

A pair of Mary-Kate and Ashley look-alikes in denim microminis hugged each other and started jumping up and down. "That's Shane! That's Shane Rockett! I think I'm gonna faint!" one of them said, pulling out a camera. "I think I'm gonna die!" her twin sister yelled, elbowing her aside for a better look.

"That's not Shane, that's just one of those celebrity look-alikes," a guy muttered from behind me. "Shane Rockett is much taller than that, and look, his hair's not even the right color. This is so bogus!" he proclaimed. "Hey you! You're a fake!" he yelled.

I couldn't stand it one more second. I spun around to glare at him and saw that he was a skinny, homely guy in torn jeans and a baseball cap. He looked at me, his eyes hard and challenging, while his date pointed at me and giggled. "And look at the chick with him! She is so FOB. Are we supposed to believe she's a movie star, too?" I quickly turned away, my cheeks flaming, my spirits wilting. I knew FOB meant "fresh off the bus."

Shane had always warned me that fans could be nasty and insulting and the best thing to do was just ignore them. I still couldn't believe that perfect strangers felt free to make horrible remarks about someone they didn't even know, and decided that if this was what fame is like, I didn't want any part of it.

"Shane, my man! What are you doing in this part of town?" The bouncer from the door had finally muscled his way through the crowd to reach us, and was pumping Shane's hand, giving a wide grin. He was wearing a Harley T-shirt with black jeans and had a thick Brooklyn accent, which seemed oddly out of place in Tinseltown.

"Adriana set something up, some sort of last-minute thing she didn't bother telling me about," Shane said curtly, pushing me in front of him. "This is Jessie," he said, practically shouting to be heard, and the bouncer nodded to me. "Get us inside as fast as you can, okay, Roy? Things are getting kind of crazy out here."

"Yeah, it's a jungle here tonight," Roy said. "I saw Adriana come in earlier, she's sitting in the back, but she didn't mention anything about your stopping by." He seemed oblivious to the earsplitting din around him and casually adjusted the earpiece on his headset.

"Yeah, it's Shane, all right," he said, speaking into the headset. "I'm bringing him in now. Get a couple of people at the door to stand by. And once we get inside, don't let anyone else in, okay? We're filled to the max anyway."

A squeal went up from a handful of girls at the edge of the rope line, and one of them reached across and grabbed Shane's sleeve while the others looked on enviously. "Shane! Shane! I love you! Can I have your autograph?" A skinny blonde leaned over with a pussycat smile. "Forget the autograph! Can I have your baby?"

"Hurry up, man," Shane said irritably. "Geez, I can't believe this group." He yanked his arm away from a sexy brunette who'd dug her long red fingernails into his upper arm and then he frowned at a girl crouching on the sidewalk at his feet. "Oh, man," he said in a disgusted voice. "Would you look at this?" The girl had managed to duck under the rope and was busily snaking her way up Shane's leg, climbing him as if he were a tree, reaching for his belt buckle. Roy grabbed her by the back of her shirt, and in one swift movement, pulled her off Shane and pushed her back into the crowd.

"Stay back there!" he bellowed at her. "I don't want to have you arrested."

"Have *me* arrested? What are you talking about? Hey, you can't rough me up, you big gorilla!" she yelled, rubbing her arm.

Roy ignored her and turned to us. "Let's go, guys. If we don't make our move now, we'll never get inside."

"Couldn't we just go back to the car?" I asked, fighting down a wave of panic. I get claustrophobic in crowds and the noise and the mass of people was starting to get to me.

"That wouldn't help, it would be just as hard, darlin'," Shane said. "And we'd have them on our tail every step of the way. Believe me, I've been through this before and it's safer to keep on going straight ahead. Don't worry, we'll get in there. Once we get behind the glass doors, we'll be fine."

Roy cleared a path, grabbing me with one beefy hand and swinging his arm like a lethal weapon in front of the crowd. By now, everyone knew Shane was on the scene, and the crowd was going wild, surging forward, threatening to engulf us. Roy was having trouble making progress, because every time we took a step forward, a solid wall of people pushed into us, knocking us back two steps. It was like battling a giant riptide; it seemed to become more powerful with each new wave, and I could feel my knees start to buckle. *How much longer would this go on?*

"Hey, Shane, why didn't you let us know you were coming? I would have had extra guys on tonight." Roy's face was grim and determined as he shouldered on ahead of us, moving his massive bulk from side to side to protect us from the squealing fans. His words were almost drowned out by the high-pitched shrieks and I could feel the start of a major headache slicing through my brain.

"Adriana," Shane muttered. "It's all her doing. She set up the whole thing and I just went along with it." He stopped to disengage himself from a girl who'd tucked her foot around his ankle and was trying to take him down, karate-style, onto the sidewalk.

"Shane, be careful!" I cried, feeling his fingers slip out of mine.

"Hey!" he said, as he nearly stumbled into the crowd. "What are you, a ninja? Quit that!" He turned to me. "Did you see that? That crazy chick thinks she's Bruce Lee!"

"Shane! Shane! Shane!" The noise was deafening, and the crowd was growing as more and more people rushed over to see what all the commotion was about. Roy kept a firm grip on me, nearly dragging me to the entrance of the club, and finally managed to push me through the glass doors. I wasn't even sure Shane was still behind me until I felt his hand grab my elbow.

"Head straight to the back to the VIP room," Shane said, panting a little. "I remember this place now—it used to have a different name. Sweetbriar, or something."

"The VIP room?" I said, groping my way past the tables and chairs that were jammed together.

"Yeah, it's a little section where no one can bother us. They have heavy security and it's always cordoned off. Better than the mob scene out front," he said wryly.

"I'll take your word for it."

The club was smoky and dark and had a tiny dance floor with some retro strobe lights that lit up the scene in garish colors and then plunged it into inky blackness. Some band I had never heard of was playing grunge rock and a woman dressed in black cargo pants and a white silk blouse slashed open to the waist swooped down on us.

"Shane, darling! I knew you'd make it!" I knew without asking that it was Adriana. She ignored me and triple air-kissed Shane, Hollywood style, as we slid into a red leather banquette. Shane edged over a little as Adriana squeezed in next to him without asking, and then ordered peach cosmopolitans all around.

"Make that a diet Coke for me," I said quickly.

"And who is your little friend?" Adriana said, her green eyes flicking over me. She was sexy in a predatory way, and I had the feeling she could be lethal if she wanted to be. She had long black hair that cascaded straight down her back and I noticed she was sitting way too close to Shane. The booth was small, and Adriana was determined to make the most of it.

"This is Jessie Phillips," Shane said, his dark eyes flashing. "She's new in town, and I think you'll be seein' a lot of her."

"Really." She gave a sardonic little twist to her lips. "Lots of girls are new in town, Shane. You of all people should know that! You're practically a one-man welcoming committee. They hop right off the bus and into your arms, don't they?"

She laughed, leaning over the table to grasp Shane's forearm. The silk blouse gaped open dangerously, giving us a view that went straight down to her waist. I was happy to see that Shane didn't even bother to take a peek.

"Jessie's a new entertainment columnist for *Juicy*." He let that sink in while Adriana blanched and seemed to shrink before my eyes. "You have heard of the hottest new magazine in town, right?" Shane continued in a hard voice. "I mean, you're a publicist. A highly paid publicist, Adriana. So I'd be right to assume that this is all part of your job, right? To be up on these things?"

"I—well, of course, you know I'm up on things, Shane," she stammered. "I've heard about *Juicy*, the Edgar Harrison publication. It's gotten a lot of buzz. I think it's going to be really hot. Really, really hot!"

Poor Adriana. You could almost see her mind scurrying like a furry rodent, trying to figure out a way to put a good spin on things. Shane was staring at her coolly, one eyebrow cocked, and I sat motionless, waiting to see what she would say next.

She smiled at me, flashing a set of perfectly bonded teeth. I flashed on an image of a very well-groomed shark with a nice set of caps. "Adriana Leone," she said, extending her hand. "It's a pleasure to meet you, Jessie, and I look forward to working with you." She paused, glancing nervously at Shane. "Do you know what you'll be assigned to? Movies or television? Models or maybe the teen market? We rep people in all those areas, and I could provide interviews or photo ops with a whole A-list roster of clients."

"I don't know yet," I said truthfully. "I don't start work until next week. As far as I know, I'm going to be doing general reporting on the entertainment industry. I think I'll cover everything, but especially the teen market."

"I see," she said, checking out my hair, my clothes, and my makeup in one quick sweep. "I'd be very happy to go over some story ideas with you." In a town where access is everything, Adriana thought she had just latched onto the sweetest deal in her life.

I just bet you would, I thought, locking eyes with Shane. I could see that it would be very easy to become cynical, living in Hollywood.

"Edgar says that Jessie has a great take on the latest trends," Shane said firmly. "And I know he plans to make the most of her talents. I think he'll give her free rein so she'll be able to write any kind of column she wants." The pride in his voice made my heart thump and I smiled at him. It was good to have one friend in a town that was filled with two-faced people who smiled in your face while they stabbed you in the back.

"Well, if I can help you in any way, don't hesitate to call," Adriana said with fake sincerity. She reached into her tiny metallic clutch bag to grab a business card, then shoved it into my hand. "I'll be glad to show you the ropes. This can be a tough town for a newcomer."

I nearly laughed aloud at the sudden transformation. Now that Adriana realized I could be valuable to her, she was pulling out all the stops, turning on the charm, acting like we were going to be best buds!

"I'd love to take you to lunch," she said, whipping out a day planner the size of the Greater Los Angeles phone book. "How does next week look?"

"It looks really jammed," I said, realizing I could play the same Hollywood power game. "You know what it's like," I said, putting a world-weary tone into my voice. "A new job, a new boss, and a full load at work. From what Edgar says, I've got to hit the ground running and offer some pitches at an editorial meeting on my very first day." I smiled. "So I doubt I'll have a second to eat lunch, but thanks anyway."

"Oh, well, let's wait until you have some slack time." I figured Adriana was probably used to being rebuffed and she turned her full attention back to Shane, staring deep into his eyes as if he were the most exciting man on the planet. When she signaled the waiter for another round of drinks, Shane caught my eye and gave me a sexy wink. I think he was amused that I had managed to put Adriana in her place right off the bat.

The two of them talked business for a few more minutes while I sipped my soda, looking around the darkened room. The VIP room was isolated from the gawking tourists outside and offered a certain amount of privacy. I recognized what Shane would call "B-list" celebrities at the bar—a failed sitcom star, a former child actor who was doing guest shots on television shows, and a fifty-something actress who did late-night infomercials for a gadget to trim your waist.

I still didn't know why Adriana had asked Shane to make an appearance, unless it was to keep the club owner happy, a short, bald man who stopped by the table and snapped our picture. I noticed that Adriana leaned into Shane, so close that their heads were nearly touching. Then the owner traded places with Adriana and posed with Shane, who looked bored with the whole game. I was glad to be left out of the whole charade, and wondered when we could leave.

"Ready to go?" Shane said a few minutes later, touching my hand. "There's still time for that walk on the beach I promised you."

"I'd like that," I said, jumping up. More air kisses from Adriana (just a double one this time, European style) and we made our way past the bar, toward the front door. Roy appeared out of the smoky darkness and offered to get the car, but Shane declined. I think he was as eager to escape the Blue Lotus as I was. I glanced at my watch and felt a little buzz of happiness; it wasn't very late, and we still could have some time together.

Shane moved ahead of me to push open the heavy glass door and that's when all hell broke loose.

"There he is! Shane, over here! Over here!" The paparazzi were out in full force, waiting for us. I stepped through the door and they descended like a pack of predatory birds, perched on top of cars, pushing against the rope line, elbowing aside the tourists to get a good shot. I heard the distinctive *pop-pop-pop* of a million flashbulbs going off at once as we stepped into the balmy night air. I stumbled forward, caught off balance, blinded by the white-hot lights. I was disoriented, surrounded by shouts and explosions of light. It was like stepping into a war zone.

"Oh man, why didn't I listen to Roy?" Shane muttered. "C'mon, Jess, we're gonna have to run for it."

"Hey, look over here, honey! Just a smile, that's all I want." An overweight guy with a video camera balanced on his shoulder was panting heavily as he ran along next to me. "Look this way, sweetie! C'mon, just one smile, it's not gonna kill you!"

I flinched and ducked my head, putting up a hand to shield my face. When the man tried to grab my arm, Shane roughly pushed him away, and picked up the pace. We were running down the uneven sidewalk, and I heard the photographer howling, "You can't touch me, I'll sue you!"

Shane gritted his teeth, tightening his grip on my hand, as we finally made it back to the Jag. He opened the doors with the remote and we tumbled inside just in time. Suddenly we were surrounded by a dozen photographers, their faces and cameras pressed up against the tinted windows, cursing that they couldn't get a shot. I felt a wave of claustrophobia come over me and my stomach churned as I leaned forward and put my face in my lap.

"Shane, get us out of here!" I said urgently. "Now!" Panic bubbled inside me as someone tried the door handle and I jumped at the sound of a sharp rapping noise on the glass window. I looked up and it seemed like there was a solid wall of people out there, all clamoring to get inside. My heart was beating so fast, I thought it was going to jump out of my chest, and beads of sweat started to pop out on my forehead. I covered my face with my hands, wishing I could make the world go away. I had never felt so frightened in my life. "Please, Shane!" I said, my voice choked with emotion.

"I'll get us out of here, darlin', don't you worry," he muttered, turning the key. "I hope they know enough to move when I start the engine." The Jag sprang to life and everyone backed off as Shane gunned the engine and then streaked down the street. Two of them tried to follow us on motorcycles but gave up the chase after a few blocks, realizing they couldn't keep up with the high-performance engine in the powerful Jag.

We headed west on Wilshire and I realized Shane was probably going to make good on his promise of a moonlight walk on the beach. But the idea of a romantic stroll in Malibu had lost its enchantment for me. The stress of the evening had gotten to me, and all I wanted to do was go home and curl up under the comforter in Ellie's guest bedroom. I decided I better speak up quickly.

"Shane, I think I'd like to go back to Ellie's, if that's okay. We can go to the beach another time." I was surprised at the wobble in my voice. Maybe I wasn't cut out to be the girlfriend of a major star after all, I thought ruefully. If tonight was any indication, life in the fast lane wasn't all it was cracked up to be.

"Are you sure? Because it's all over, Jess, really it is." His voice was ragged with concern. "Nobody's on our tail," he added, glancing in the rearview mirror. "You can take a look and see for yourself." He gave a short laugh. "They're eatin' our dust, I promise you. The evenin's still young and we can have some time to spend alone together." When I remained silent, he glanced over, his eyes dark and serious. "But if you're sure that's what you want," he said hesitantly, "I'll take you back home, darlin'."

"I'm sure." I took a deep breath, willing myself to calm down. I managed a weak smile. "I'm sorry, Shane, but I just think I'm ready to call it a night, that's all. I hope you understand." Deep down, I wondered if he ever could understand. Wouldn't Heidi Hopkins or any of the other Hollywood hotties take something like this in stride? I flashed on a sudden image of Heidi, the blond beauty from *Reckless Summer*. She certainly wouldn't have let a pack of paparazzi get to her. Knowing Heidi, she'd bat those baby blues and vamp her way down the sidewalk, loving every minute of it.

"You can't let those vultures get to you, Jess. If you let yourself be bothered by it, they win. The trick is to try to live your life as normally as you can."

"I'll try to remember that," I said in a thready voice. "And I'm sure you're absolutely right. But it's going to take me some time to get used to all this, Shane. I don't know how you deal with being hounded by the press all the time. Do you get attacked every time you go out?" I looked down at my forearm. A large, purplish bruise was already forming, and I couldn't even remember how I got it. An overly enthusiastic fan? Or being corralled by Roy as we made our way to the door?

"Only if they recognize me," Shane said in his deep voice. "That's why I usually have a wall of people around me. This last-minute stuff, like tonight, just isn't a good idea. That's when things go wrong." He waited until we pulled up in front of Ellie's to place his hand on the back of my neck and pull me in for a dizzying kiss. "I'm sorry this happened, Jess. I never expected the night to turn out this way." He nuzzled my ear, his lips warm and soft. "Things are different out here, you'll find that out soon enough. Nothing is easy, like it was back in Bedford."

"I know, Shane," I told him. "You told me it goes with the territory. It's not your fault." I kissed him back, melting a little, just looking into those amazing dark eyes flecked with gold. Shane was absolutely right. Things *were* different out here. But I couldn't help but wonder—was the Hollywood fast track going to derail our relationship?

* * *

EARLY THE NEXT MORNING, I WOKE TO THE MELLOW SOUNDS OF Norah Jones drifting through the condo and found Tracy and Ellie huddled over the Sunday papers. The kitchen was splattered with bright California sunshine pouring in from the sliding glass doors, and I spotted an open box of Krispy Kremes on the counter.

I had tiptoed in late last night, and hadn't had a chance to tell Tracy about my experience with Shane at Blue Lotus and the onslaught of the paparazzi. Or Adriana the publicist, and the way she had seemed a little too cozy with Shane. It was just business, wasn't it? And she was joking when she said Shane was a "one-man welcoming committee" for new girls in town, wasn't she?

I shoved the image from my mind. This was no time to let my imagination run haywire, I reminded myself. I had plenty of time to learn the ropes and I'd be running into dozens of people just as predatory as Adriana. Shane was right. I'd just have to meet each challenge head-on and not let these experiences drag me down or make me doubt myself.

I yawned and shook my head, trying to dispel the frightening images of the paparazzi reaching for us, shouting at us, chasing us all the way back to the Jag and pounding on the windows. I wished I could magically erase those scenes from my memory banks, but I knew that wasn't possible. I'd have to get a grip and deal with them if I was going to work in a high-profile job for the hottest new magazine in this town.

Tracy was smiling like someone who knew a tantalizing secret. "Jess!" she squealed. "We've been waiting for you to wake up! You're famous."

"I am?" I grabbed a lemon-filled donut with a dusting of powdered sugar and decided to play along. "Gee, maybe I'll be the next Lindsay Lohan. Or do you think I'm more the Rachel Bilson type? Maybe with the right eye makeup, but I don't think I'll ever get that great hair, do you?" I vamped a little in my T-shirt and sweatpants, pretending to be posing for the camera.

"Jess, I'm not kidding. You made the entertainment section of the *L.A. Times*. Look, here's your picture!"

"Let her wake up first," Ellie said gently. She pushed a cup of steaming cappuccino at me as I hopped onto a stool at the breakfast bar, tucking my bare feet through the rungs at the bottom.

"I'm really in the paper?" I suddenly flashed on the image of the paparazzi chasing us down the street last night, clicking away, flashbulbs popping. I hadn't realized the pictures would make the morning edition; all I had thought about was escaping the photographers.

"In two different sections," Ellie said. "The pictures from the Blue Lotus are in the entertainment section, but you've also got a mention in one of the gossip columns. Have your coffee first, I know you came in late. There may be more pictures in the tabloids, we can check on that later." She shot me an appraising look, and there was something about her thoughtful expression that made me think that I wouldn't be thrilled by the coverage.

"The tabloids? I didn't even think of that," I muttered. I wondered if my face was going to be splashed all over the papers in the checkout aisle at the supermarkets back in Bedford. *Jessie and her fifteen minutes of fame*, people would probably think.

"That must have been some mob scene last night," Tracy said, pushing the paper at me. "There's a nice shot of the two of you. You should send it to your mom."

Ellie nodded. "I think so too. Of course, one of the wire services will probably pick it up and they'll print it in your hometown paper, Jess. After all, this will be big news to the folks back home. But we can make copies, if you like. I'm sure your friends in Bedford would be thrilled to see what you're doing in Hollywood."

"Hmm, I'm not so sure of that. Not everyone," I said, thinking of Alexis Bright, Fairmont Academy drama queen. I had beaten her out for the part opposite Shane in *Reckless Summer* and I don't think she was ever going to let me forget it. "Let me see what it looks like first." I never like pictures of myself, and I crossed my fingers, hoping I looked good.

"Here you go." Tracy passed me the paper and I groaned. Shane, as always, looked awesome, very Hollywood, standing on the front steps of the club. I had a deer-in-the-headlights look, as if I was quivering with anxiety, ready to bolt back into the forest. And the dress that I had thought was so amazing in the store? It didn't really work well on camera, I realized with a sigh. Instead of making me look tall and willowy, the gauzy silk fabric billowed out in the midsection, like the jib on a Flying Scot.

I could see why movie stars paid big bucks to "stylists" to get them ready to face photographers. It was hard to know what kind of styles and fabrics would photograph well, without a ton of experience. Since looking good was their business, starlets were always glad to go to the experts. I had relied on my own instincts and it had been a mistake. Lesson learned.

"Aaargh. This isn't a very flattering picture," I said slowly. "And look at this caption. They're calling me an 'unidentified companion.' That sounds like somebody he just met."

"Well, what else could they call you?" Tracy said reasonably. "Nobody knew your name, and besides, you both hightailed it out of there so fast, there wasn't time to answer any questions."

"What does the other piece say? Am I really mentioned in a gossip column? Just so long as there isn't another picture." I figured I better get everything over with at once, and since I was going to be writing an entertainment column myself, it would be interesting to see how I was portrayed.

Ellie wordlessly pushed the paper at me, her expression blank. Not a good sign, I decided. I quickly scanned it and saw my name in boldface. "At least they spelled my name right," I said bitingly. "I suppose it could be worse, right?" I gave a nervous little laugh and started to read aloud. " 'The *Hollywood Insider* has uncovered some very hot dish about teen heartthrob Shane Rockett. He has a new main squeeze and it's Jessie Phillips, his co-star from *Reckless Summer.*'" I put down the coffee cup with a sharp thump on the granite counter. "Now I'm being referred to as his main squeeze? That's even worse than 'unidentified companion.' Wait till my mom reads this." I groaned. "I just hope this column doesn't make it to the papers back east. Nobody'll believe it."

Just for a second, I flashed on Marc LaPierre, my on-again, off-again boyfriend down in New Orleans. It's doubtful he would read the Hollywood trade papers, but what if the story got picked up by one of the news syndicates? He was still expecting me to visit him in a week or so, and I had put off calling to tell him about my change of plans.

"Um, there's more," Tracy said, wincing a little. "You probably should read the next paragraph." She and Ellie exchanged a sympathetic look and it was obvious that they knew what was coming up.

I never could have predicted the bomb that was about to be dropped on me. I turned the page, scanned the rest of the column, and my heart sank as I read the rest of the item. " 'This new love interest will certainly be a surprise to Heidi Hopkins, who was seen playing kissy-face with Shane at the Ivy the other night. What a difference a day makes!' "

I put the paper down and looked at Tracy. "What a difference a day makes?" I repeated angrily. "I can't believe this! So Shane was at the Ivy with Heidi?" *And not only was he with her, but playing kissy-face!* I thought, my cheeks flaming. *How humiliating!*

"It sure looks that way," Tracy said, inspecting her fingernails. "I thought you said he had a business meeting." Tracy never wanted to criticize Shane in front of me, but I bet she had already filled Ellie in on the whole episode with Heidi Hopkins a few weeks ago. To say that I had a "trust issue" with Shane was an understatement. He was the most exciting guy I had ever met, but sometimes he played a little loose with the truth, and he had a tendency to tell people what he thought they wanted to hear. Maybe it was the actor in him? Or maybe it was just Shane.

"That's exactly what he called it, a business meeting. He insisted we leave Venice Beach so he could meet with his agent and some producers about a film project. He drove back here like a maniac so he could race off to the Ivy." I shook my head in disbelief, becoming more outraged by the minute. When would I learn that with Shane, nothing is what it seems?

"Did you ask him about it? How the meeting went?" Tracy asked in a neutral voice. She was obviously making an effort to keep her opinions about Shane to herself.

"I sure did, and he said it was a big nothing, a waste of time. That the film deal was a real back-burner project and would probably never see the light of day." I winced when I thought of the warmth and sincerity in his dark eyes during that conversation. How could I have been so stupid? How could I have let myself be so blinded by his charm again?

"He never mentioned Heidi Hopkins?" Ellie asked gently.

"Not a word. Believe me, I would have noticed if he had. And I would have asked him about it." I drained my cappuccino and stared out at the sunlight bouncing off the wrought-iron railing on Ellie's balcony. A few minutes earlier, I had felt happy inside, looking at the sparkling Pacific topped with whitecaps, the robin's-egg-blue sky, and the expanse of white sandy beach below.

I had thought this was going to be the start of another perfect California day.

Now everything had changed, my blinders were off, and I could have kicked myself for trusting the sexy, charming, and oh-so-dangerous Shane Rockett one more time.

Chapter Seven

BEFORE I KNEW IT, THE NEXT MORNING HAD ROLLED AROUND, and I was reporting to work at the *Juicy* offices on Wilshire Boulevard. Tracy and I had been up at the crack of dawn, completely psyched at the prospect of landing two of the hottest jobs in town. We had changed our outfits at least half a dozen times.

Ellie insisted on driving both of us there for our first day, even though it meant battling rush-hour traffic in downtown Los Angeles to get us there on time. She said she had to do some errands in town, anyway, but I think she was just trying to make things as easy as possible for us.

* * *

EDGAR HARRISON OFFERED TO DRIVE US HOME THAT EVENING, because he wanted to stop in and see one of Ellie's watercolors. Shane's mom, Lily, ever the matchmaker, had insisted that one of Ellie's delicate pastels would be perfect in the lobby of *Juicy*. Thinking of Lily Rockett reminded me of Shane and I mentally warned myself to push the thought aside. It was just too upsetting to deal with at the moment.

I was glad that I had a busy day ahead of me, because I knew I couldn't face talking to Shane and I still hadn't made that phone call to Marc in New Orleans. I had so many unanswered questions and my thoughts were swirling. Was Shane really making out with Heidi that night at the Ivy? Or was it just vicious gossip from someone who wanted to sell papers?

Was Marc still counting on me coming to New Orleans, and had he seen the pictures of me with Shane outside the Blue Lotus? Was this finally a deal breaker in our relationship? Had Marc's feelings for me changed, or was he as true blue as ever?

And what were my feelings for the fabulous Shane Rockett, now that he had deceived me once again? Or had he? And why was I so hesitant to ask him? Was I really so afraid of the answer he might give me?

My love life had suddenly gotten more complicated than one of the plots on *The* O.C. and I knew it was time to call a time-out. Look at the bright side, I told myself. It was a bright sunny day, I was starting a red-hot job in Hollywood, and I was going to have the best summer of my life. So I took a deep breath and made a resolution as we headed down Rodeo Drive, passing Gucci, Chanel, and all the other trendy shops lining the famous street. For the next eight hours, I would focus on my work, do an awesome job for Edgar, and put guys—all guys— out of my head!

"This traffic is unbelievable," Tracy said, eyeing the bumper-to-bumper cars turning onto Wilshire. I glanced over at Tracy. We had both dressed carefully in linen pencil skirts, crisp white blouses, and low-heeled pumps. Ellie had said that the dress code for *Juicy* was "business casual," and suggested we dress conservatively until we had a feeling for what the other interns would be wearing.

"Pretty amazing, isn't it?" Ellie said cheerfully. She deftly changed lanes while sipping a caramel macchiato we had picked up at Starbucks a few minutes earlier. "The funny thing is, you get used to it," she went on, as if she could read my mind. "You really do. When I first moved out here, I thought it was overwhelming and nearly moved to Pasadena, but now it's just part of my life. I've got books on tape, and all my music. Plus I do some of my best thinking in the car." She turned to look at us, her Gucci sunglasses pushed up on her hair. "So how are you doing? All set for your first day?"

I nodded. "I feel like I'm back in third grade," I said, trying to quiet the butterflies swirling in my stomach.

"I'm a basket case," Tracy said. "I thought I'd never fall asleep last night. And when I finally did doze off, I dreamt I walked into *Juicy* stark naked. I had forgotten to get dressed!"

"Oh, no!" Ellie hooted. "A classic anxiety dream. I know how you feel," she went on sympathetically. "I feel exactly the same way when I meet a client for the first time and have to show them my portfolio. Will they like me? Will they appreciate my work? Will they want to hire me? That queasy feeling never goes away. Maybe it's just as well; I think it gives you an edge."

I raised my eyebrows. "Funny, Shane said the same thing," I murmured. Ellie didn't answer and I could have kicked myself for breaking my own rule. *No Shane today*, I repeated silently, like a mantra. Now if I could just find a way to go five minutes without thinking of him! I thought ruefully.

"WELCOME, GIRLS!" A BEAUTIFUL ASIAN GIRL WEARING A PALE yellow Marc Jacobs dress greeted us as soon as we stepped off the elevator. I recognized the dress, a flirty little number with cap sleeves and a dropped waistline, because Ellie had pointed it out to me at a boutique on Montana Avenue. Not only did I remember the dress, but I remembered the price tag: a cool one thousand dollars.

"I'm Laura Li," she said, extending her hand, "and I'm one of the senior vice presidents of *Juicy*." She smiled at both of us. "Jessie and Tracy, right?" she said, nodding at each of us in turn. She was drop-dead gorgeous with flawless skin, sparkling dark eyes, and straight jet-black hair that cascaded down her back like a waterfall.

"That's us," I said, a little nervously. *Marc Jacobs?* If this was "business casual," what did she wear for a night out on the town? I remembered Ellie saying that power lunches were very big in L.A., so maybe she had scheduled a lunch date at some fabulous place like Chaya or "the Bev," which is shorthand for the Beverly Hills Hotel. I suddenly felt very FOB, as the nasty fan at the Blue Lotus had described it.

I glanced down and noticed that my linen skirt had already started to wrinkle and my crisp white blouse had wilted a little during the ride into town. It was hard not to feel insecure next to this beautiful girl who could have stepped out of the pages of *Vogue.* As Ellie had warned me, the standards were different in L.A. and perfection was everywhere. My mother had always insisted that looks aren't everything, but I was having trouble reminding myself of that. It seemed that in L.A., looks really *were* everything and perfection was the name of the game.

"Edgar described you perfectly. Welcome aboard! Follow me, please," Laura said, briskly, whisking us past the long marble reception desk to a labyrinth of hallways. "Your office is down this way, Jessie. Tracy, as soon as we drop Jessie off, I'll take you down to the photo department."

We obediently trotted after her, hurrying down a long narrow corridor lined with cubicles like something out of a *Doonesbury* cartoon. "She doesn't look old enough to be vice president of the senior class, much less a major magazine," Tracy whispered.

"I know. And she must make oodles of money," I said, eyeing her shoes. Sling-back lemon-yellow Jimmy Choos. Sarah Jessica Parker had worn a pair just like them on a date with Mr. Big in *Sex and the City*.

"This is your spot," Laura said, making a sharp turn into a cramped office with no windows. I noticed there were four old-fashioned metal desks with scuffed green tops, the kind you see on cop shows like *Law & Order*. "It looks a little crowded at the moment," she said, noticing my expression, "but once we get these boxes out of here, it will open right up."

"It looks fine," I said, hoping I sounded more enthusiastic than I felt. I locked eyes with Tracy, who was giving me an "I can't believe this" look behind Laura's back. "I'm sure I'll settle in perfectly." I forced a smile, and Laura looked relieved.

"And you won't be all alone in here," she said brightly, as a sullen-looking red-haired girl appeared, carrying a diet soda. "Alicia will be sharing the office with you, and we're expecting two more interns tomorrow. Both females. It'll be fun," she promised.

"Yeah, it'll be just like a sleepover," Alicia said sarcastically. "Maybe we can exchange makeup tips and give each other French manicures."

Laura's eyes widened a little at Alicia's comment, and she flapped her delicate hands nervously, obviously eager to make her getaway. "Well, I'll leave you two to get acquainted, and I'll take Tracy down to her office. I'll be back later to take you to Personnel to get all the paperwork squared away, Jessie."

"Meet me for lunch, Trace?" I said quickly, as Laura speed-walked out the door.

"I'll be back at twelve," Tracy promised. She glanced at the phone on my desk. "Call me, if you can figure out where I am." She galloped after Laura, who had already disappeared down the corridor, her expensive shoes beating out a staccato on the oversized Italian tiles.

"Alicia Reynolds," my office mate said, throwing herself into her battered desk chair and swigging her soda. "You've got to be Jessie Phillips."

I nodded. "And that was my friend, Tracy, who's headed for the photo department," I said helpfully.

"I know. Lucy Liu told us all about you." She foraged in her purse for an energy bar and broke it in half. "Want a piece?"

"No thanks," I said quickly. "Lucy Liu?"

Alicia's face twisted in a smile. "Laura Li. She's got the Lucy Liu thing going, don't you think? Any day now, I expect her to come in here dressed in a tight black leather jumpsuit and practice some karate kicks on Edgar." She chortled at the idea.

"She seems nice," I said hesitantly.

Alicia snorted. "Hah! You've got a lot to learn. Stick around. You'll find out nobody's nice here." She paused. "You know Edgar, right?"

I nodded. "I met him very briefly at a party." For some reason, I decided to leave Shane out of the conversation, figuring that the less Alicia knew about me, the better.

She pondered this, checking me out, chewing noisily on her granola bar. "Well, maybe in social situations, he's okay. But he's a monster to work for. Take my word for it, he's a real prima donna."

"Oh, I had no idea. I only talked to him for a few minutes." I didn't know what to say. I certainly didn't want to bad-mouth Edgar, who had offered me a job and made it possible for me to stay in Hollywood, but I also didn't want to antagonize Alicia, who seemed to know the ropes. I figured she would be good to know and she could guide me through the power structure at *Juicy*. Plus there was something about the sardonic twist to her mouth and her hard eyes that made me think she would make a very dangerous enemy. The last thing I wanted to do was get on her bad side.

"So how did you get started here?" I said, wondering if we could ever be friends.

"Hah! That's an easy one." She swept a pile of manila folders from her desk to the floor before answering me. "My dad's one of the major investors in this rag. And he got the bright idea that I should have a summer job before starting college next fall, so he strong-armed Edgar into giving me an internship. At least, that's what he told me." She paused, expecting me to say something.

"But that's not the real reason?" I prompted, wondering why she was telling me all this.

"Of course not." She gave a grating laugh. "That's the first thing you've got to learn out here, Jessie. No one ever tells you the real reason for anything. The truth is never what it seems." She waited, and when I didn't take the bait, she added, "So, the real reason is that my parents are going through what they call a 'messy' divorce and I think they both wanted me out of their hair. It's like that movie with Brad Pitt and Angelina Jolie, you know, the one where they're both assassins, and they try to kill each other?"

I nodded. I had seen *Mr. and Mrs. Smith* the first week it came out. "It must be tough on you," I murmured.

"Well, you gotta roll with the punches, you know?" She paused to inspect her fingernails and I noticed they were bitten down to the quick. "Maybe it will be easier when Dad moves out. He's getting a condo over in Santa Monica, so Mom and I will be alone in the house. Not that I'm really looking forward to spending quality time with Mom. When she has too much vodka and cran, she likes to tell me all this really personal stuff about their marriage. It creeps me out. I feel like screaming, TMI! TMI!"

I waited for her to explain, and she added, "Too much information. Don't you use that expression? Where are you *from*, anyway?"

I sighed. I seemed to spend a lot of time explaining myself in L.A. "A little town in Connecticut, a place you've never heard of. It's called Bedford." She gave me a blank look as if I had just said I was from Mars. "It's nice, really."

She stopped eating her power bar and scrunched up her face. "Bedford? Hmmm, why does that sound familiar? That's not part of the Hamptons, is it? That really hot place where Paris Hilton has a summer home? They had a party there and they shot the whole thing for the E! channel. Paris and Nicky looked really hot and I think there's lots of celebs who live there. So that's where you're from, huh? Do you hang out with Paris and her friends?"

I smiled, thinking that Angelenos seemed to know nothing about the geography of the East Coast. "No, it's not part of the Hamptons. It's not even close to the Hamptons. It's just a little town, very quiet—"

Alicia suddenly rocked forward, snapping her desk chair upright with a sharp crack. "Wait a minute. Bedford! Now I know why I heard of it!" she said. "That's where they shot that Shane Rockett flick, Restless something-or-other. I never could figure out why they picked that little hick town. And I heard he had mostly nobodies for co-stars, except of course for the fabulous Heidi Hopkins." She raised her eyebrows and said Heidi's name in a mocking voice. "I bet it's going to be one of those straight-to-video flicks," she said, giving another harsh laugh. "I think I'll get it for laughs when it comes out at Blockbuster."

"Reckless Summer," I corrected her wearily. I had only been around Alicia for twenty minutes, and already I felt exhausted. She was an emotional vampire, sucking all the life and enthusiasm out of me with her constant sarcasm and Kelly Osborne

moodiness. At the rate we were going, it was going to be a very long summer.

"Are you sure?" she said challengingly. I could see that Alicia didn't like to have anyone disagree with her.

"I know for sure it's called *Reckless Summer*," I repeated. I decided it was better to get the truth out right now, in the beginning. Alicia was bound to find out anyway. "And, actually, I was *in* that movie. With Shane Rockett."

Alicia's jaw dropped. "You're kidding!" She looked me over, taking in my good-girl outfit: linen skirt (already wrinkled) and tailored white blouse (wilted from the ride into the city). "Wow, I'd kill to be in a movie with him. He is so hot! He is . . . beyond hot!" she added, waving her arms helplessly as if words failed her. "Who would ever think you'd get a chance like that, and all because you live in some little burg way out in the sticks! Some people have all the luck."

I wanted to tell her that I didn't think of my hometown as a "little burg," and that there was more to getting the role than just being in the right place at the right time, but the phone rang then, and Alicia grabbed it on the first ring. "Duty calls," she said, picking up a sheaf of papers and heading out the door. "We'll talk more later. I want to hear all about what it was like being in a movie with Shane." She paused at the doorway to shoot me another look, shaking her head in disbelief. The message was plain: how did someone like me, a nobody from a hick town, ever get lucky enough to be in a movie with a hot star like Shane?

The morning dragged on as Laura (who I nearly called "Lucy") returned to take me to Personnel, where I met a sour-faced woman who made me fill out tons of paperwork. Edgar spotted me in the hall, raced over to pump my hand in greeting, and then disappeared so fast, I wondered if I had imagined him.

"He's always like this," Laura said with a laugh. "He operates at warp speed, and limits conversations to thirty seconds. Don't take it personally. You'll have a chance to sit down with him later in the week. He gives an orientation for all the summer interns and he really tries to get to know each of you as individuals."

"Okay, I'll try not to take it personally." I grinned at her. "But thanks for the warning. I was beginning to feel a little paranoid."

"Oh, we're a pretty friendly bunch here," she said. "Don't believe everything you hear," she added, making me think she had a pretty good handle on Alicia. "A lot of people like to pretend that this is a cutthroat town, and a dog-eat-dog business where you can't trust anybody."

I smiled. "Yeah, I think I've heard that a few times," I admitted.

"I'm sure you have, but don't believe a word of it. It's just part of the mystique that's grown up about L.A., that's all. There're some really nice people working here, and we all have jobs to do. You'll see." She gave me a warm smile and I felt my spirits lifting a little. "It'll take a few days to get adjusted, that's all. And then you'll see that I'm right."

She made a move to hurry off, but I stopped her. "Uh, Laura, I've been meaning to ask you, what do I do exactly?"

"Do?" I saw her sneak a peek at her watch.

"My job," I reminded her. "You just said that everyone has a job, but I can't figure out what I'm supposed to do."

"Well," she said hesitantly, "I think you and Alicia are covering teen stars for the moment, but I'm not sure about the specific assignments. We hired an editorial director for that department, but she's not starting until the end of the month. You'll be reporting to her as soon as she arrives; she's winding things up at another job." She glanced down at some notes on her clipboard. "But I don't want you to feel like you're left out in the cold, Jessie. Didn't Alicia fill you in? She's been here for a couple of weeks, and I think she's working on a couple of projects for Edgar."

I didn't want to be a total rat and say that Alicia had been gone most of the morning (and that she didn't seem too eager to share any information with me), so I just played dumb. "We talked a little bit, but she didn't get into the details," I said, figuring that was a safe answer.

Laura's cell phone went off, and she reached down to turn off the ringer without even glancing at the number. "That's my secretary reminding me I'm late for a staff meeting," she said apologetically. "We've got to crunch some numbers and go over the week's assignments."

"Go ahead to your meeting, I can always talk to you later," I offered.

"Thanks," she said, and then gave me a thoughtful look. "Say, would you like to come to the meeting with me? I have to clear it with Edgar, but I was just thinking that it would be a great introduction to *Juicy*. You'll get to meet everyone all at once, and you'll get an idea about what we're doing." She grinned, her eyes flashing. "And wait till you see all the hot story ideas we've got in the pipeline," she added playfully. "You'll see what an editorial meeting is really like and I bet you'll come away with loads of good ideas for your own writing."

I was stunned. "Could I really go? I'd love to!" The thought of escaping that dismal office and the depressing Alicia was so wonderful I could hardly believe it. "I don't even have a pen," I said, patting my pocket, wishing I had been more professional. "Do I have time to run back to my office?"

"Take mine." She handed me a beautiful sky-blue Mark Cross pen.

"It's beautiful," I said. "I'll give it right back after the meeting."

"No, keep it, I want you to have it," she said. "Welcome to the company, Jess."

I DIDN'T HAVE ANY IDEA WHAT TO EXPECT WHEN I WALKED INTO my first editorial meeting at *Juicy*, but I trotted like a puppy after Laura as we made our way down the labyrinth of *Juicy* offices. She finally ushered me into a beautiful conference room with floor-to-ceiling windows overlooking Wilshire Boulevard.

I chose a seat at the far end of a long rosewood table. There were bottles of Crystal Geyser and PowerBars at every seat and a silver bowl filled with frosted grapes served as a centerpiece. I wondered if the grapes were edible, or just a beautiful decoration. About a dozen people were already seated and there was an excited buzz of conversation humming around the table.

Edgar hadn't arrived yet, and Laura slid into a seat near the head of the table.

"Say hi to our new intern, everyone!" she called out. "This is Jessie Phillips, and she's going to be covering teen stars for us!" A few people paused to look up curiously, but most people stared at me blankly for a split second and then went right on with their conversations. Laura flashed me an apologetic smile, and then gave a half shrug, shaking her head. If I'd thought I was going to be the new flavor of the month here at *Juicy*, I was in for a big surprise.

I smiled back, feeling vaguely uncomfortable, and wondered if I should have tried to get Tracy an invitation to the meeting. It had all happened so fast, the thought hadn't occurred to me, but now I felt a little guilty, thinking of Tracy stuck by herself in the photo department.

Laura busied herself with a thick folder of computer printouts and I sat back, listening to snatches of a conversation between two young women in their twenties sitting across the table from me. The first one clicked her cell phone shut and said in a heated tone, "Well, that was a total waste of time! I don't believe this guy. I told his publicist he's not going to have control over my interview questions—that we don't do business that way. If he wants someone to do a puff piece, he better call someone else because we don't do that stuff at *Juicy*. Doesn't she know we're journalists, not PR flacks!"

"I'll do a puff piece if the money's right," a scruffy-looking guy piped up. He had tousled hair and was wearing a vintage rock T-shirt with faded jeans and dirty tennies. He was so far off the *Juicy* "dress code" that I figured he must be incredibly talented, or related to one of the investors.

"You won't do a puff piece *here*, Simon," the girl said pointedly. "If you want to do one, you'll have to peddle it somewhere else. I'd try the *Sunset Strip Insider*—they're always trolling for pieces—but don't let Edgar catch you doing it. And you'll have to use a phony byline or he'll fire you on the spot. If you ever bothered to read the fine print in your contract, you know we're not allowed to write for anyone else."

"You got me there, luv," he said, "I never bothered to read the fine print." I looked up in surprise. He had a deep voice with a strong cockney accent that made him sound exactly like Paul McCartney. He caught me staring and gave me a broad wink before popping a grape in his mouth. I suddenly felt shy and pretended to be writing notes on the yellow legal pad in front of me.

No puff pieces, I wrote at the top of the page. I remember

Shane telling me that a puff piece was an article designed to make the celeb look good. It was packed with easy questions, nothing hardball or controversial. All the questions sounded like they were written by someone's press agent, not a real reporter, and the answers were rehearsed. Funny how I never thought about any of this stuff until I met Shane and got involved in the business myself.

Tracy asked Shane once if he knew the questions the reporters were going to ask him before he walked into the interview. Shane had laughed, and said he couldn't figure out why an actor would insist on knowing the questions ahead of time. "That's like playin' a tennis game with someone who always lets you win, because he hits the ball right to where you're standin.' I'd rather do an interview where the reporter has something interesting to say and keeps me on my toes."

"Who are we talking about here? Who wants to control the interview?" I yanked my mind back to the present as a young guy with gold Armani sunglasses, the same kind Leonardo DiCaprio wore in *The Aviator*, leaned forward into the conversation. The young woman with the cell phone mentioned the name of an actor on a top-ranked medical drama. She kept her voice low and mouthed the name at him, her eyebrows raised.

"Oh, him? Really? I had no idea he was like that." He laughed and ripped open the wrapper on a power bar. My stomach was growling, but I held back, noticing that no one else was touching the food. "He must think he's Tom Cruise, if he thinks he's big enough to pull that off. Man, is he in for a wake-up call when Edgar finds out. You know what a control freak Edgar is; he'd never let the reporter agree to those conditions."

"And the guy actually wants control over the pictures, too," the girl said. "His publicity person said so. What an ego."

"Funny," the guy in sunglasses replied, munching away, "I never thought he'd try to pull something like that. I met him once at a charity event, and he doesn't come across like that in person. He seemed like a really nice guy. Very low-key."

"Maybe he's not the one behind this," the other girl said tentatively. "It could be Shana, his publicist; she's always impossible to work with. Do you know she actually came to a photo shoot when I worked for *Star Tracks*, and was shouting orders to the photographer? He was really ticked off, especially when she told him what gels to use. She said amber gels were the most flattering for her client's skin tones."

"You're kidding! If Jeremy was the photographer, he would have gone ballistic and stalked off the set. But first he would have given her a piece of his mind."

She laughed. "Funny you should say that, because it *was* Jeremy and that's exactly what happened! He really told her off, but luckily, she couldn't understand a word he was saying. Thank God for that thick Welsh accent of his."

"Oh, I love Jeremy, he's such a teddy bear," a thin blonde said, joining in the conversation. "I always try to hire him freelance, but I hear his rates have gone through the roof since he did that Madonna spread."

I took it all in, still pinching myself. Was this really happening? Was I really sitting in on an editorial meeting at a Hollywood entertainment magazine? I wondered if I'd ever feel like a part of the team, and realized I was still very much an outsider. Laura had gone out of her way to be friendly, but as far as everyone else was concerned, I was still Jessie from Nowheresville.

Chapter Eight

★

EDGAR WALKED IN JUST THEN, AND THE MEETING WAS OFFICIALLY called to order. I noticed all the chatter stopped while everyone jockeyed for position, like racehorses at the starting lineup. Even Scruffy Guy sat upright in his chair, giving Edgar a look of rapt attention while the assignments were handed out. Since this was an editorial meeting, not a business one, the focus was on what articles would be slated for upcoming issues, who would do the writing, and who would do the photography. I felt hopelessly out of the loop, until Edgar surprised me by actually noticing I was there.

"Jessie," he said suddenly, looking down the table. "Good to see you. I hope you're settling in well." His tone was coolly formal and professional. Even though he had joked around with me at the party, I knew I had better show him the proper respect as my boss.

"Very well, Mr. Harrison, thanks." I smiled at Laura, who was watching me intently. "Everyone's been very helpful to me."

"So far," Scruffy Guy noted, and everyone laughed. "Let's see if you still say that by the end of the week."

Even Edgar permitted himself a small chuckle before saying, "Simon is our resident comedian. I don't know what we'd do without him to lighten the mood." He gave Simon an appraising look, as if he might not be needing the services of a comedian much longer.

"Well," he said finally to Laura, "what's on the wish list? Wait a second, I want to fill Jessie in first." His careful gaze drifted over me. "Jessie, I should explain that we end every editorial meeting by going over a list of all the people we would love to interview, but haven't found a way to do it. At least, not yet. So that's why we call it the wish list." He paused, looking at Laura, and she sat up straighter, consulting her notes.

"Well, we have Madonna as a possible, as part of a segment on Kabbalah. And Julia Roberts in a feature on raising twins."

"No," Edgar said firmly. "Scratch those ideas. I don't like either one of them. Next!"

"Tom Cruise?" Laura looked hesitant. "I heard he's not doing any more interviews." She sighed.

"Put him down as a maybe," Edgar insisted. "Anybody else?"

A few more high-profile celeb names were mentioned and then a petite redhead jumped in. "Jazz!" she called out. "Jazz

Holliday. She's new, but she's gonna be the hottest thing in town when her show comes out in the fall."

"Jazz Holliday? An interesting choice," Edgar said, stroking his goatee. "Why do we want to do a piece on her? I barely know who she is. Unless I'm out of the loop." He looked around the table and gave a short bark of laughter to show he was joking. The idea of Edgar being out of the loop was as unthinkable as Harry Winston's being out of diamonds.

"Because she absolutely refuses to give interviews—" the redhead began, but Simon cut in, with a devilish expression on his face.

"So does my great-aunt Hilda, but you don't want to see her on the cover, do you?" he asked lazily. "Just because someone plays hard to get doesn't mean they're worth interviewing."

Edgar held his hand up. "Please, Simon, save your jokes for the Laugh Factory. Go ahead, Lexi, what's her story?"

Lexi's face lit up as everyone turned to stare at her. "Well, she's got the lead on that new teen show, *Bad Intentions*, but they're keeping it under wraps. I know for a fact that she's got the part, but no one will admit it. She's on a crash diet to lose fifteen pounds to fit into the clothes they've picked out for her."

"How do you know all this?" Simon asked.

"We have the same personal trainer," Lexi said impatiently. "Believe me, it's true. I saw her exercise log when Rudy accidentally left it on the counter. She's doing five hundred crunches a day and she's already as skinny as a swizzle stick. When September comes and the show takes off, she'll be a megastar." She gave a little giggle. "Assuming she can fit into her size zero wardrobe."

"Do we have an address on her?" Edgar asked.

"That's a tough one, because she's moving this week. Out of some little hotel in Venice Beach to an upscale condo in Silver Lake."

"Wow, Silver Lake? The money must be good," Scruffy Guy offered. "Maybe she really is on the fast track."

"Wait a minute, back up a little. Why are the producers keeping quiet about all this?" Laura asked. "I thought they'd be glad to have the advance publicity."

"Because they're starting this big coast-to-coast star search campaign, pretending to audition unknown actors for the part," Lexi said. "But it's all a fake. We could scoop everyone else if we could just get her to sit down to an interview. And somehow get her to admit that's she got the starring role."

"That's easier said than done," Laura said archly. "There's probably something in her contract forbidding her to talk about it. If the word ever got out, no one would bother showing up for the bogus auditions."

"Oh, I'm sure she's been sworn to secrecy," Lexi said. "But maybe we could just use a couple of comments from her, and then hint at the rest. It'll blow the star search contest sky-high, that's for sure."

Edgar nodded. "I think I remember reading about it in *Variety*. The producers are flying into all these little towns in the Midwest and the South looking for new faces." He paused. "I always wondered why anyone would think star searches are legit. They'd have to be seriously deluded to really think this is their big chance."

I ventured a question. "Why would a producer fly all over the country looking for talent, when there are thousands of unemployed actors right here in L.A.?"

"For publicity," Simon said, a sardonic smile lighting up his face. "It's all a giant publicity game. It drums up a lot of buzz about the show, and all these yahoos actually think they've got a shot at stardom." He turned to Lexi. "So how do you know Jazz is getting the part, if they're keeping the whole thing quiet? Maybe she's just some exercise freak. Everybody in L.A. is."

Lexi leaned forward. "It's more than just the exercise log," she said confidently. She paused dramatically for effect. "It just so happens that the girl who walks my dog knows the real estate agent who's working with the wardrobe mistress on the show and she mentioned that Jazz had packed on a few pounds and—"

"Stop! Stop right there!" Everyone laughed when Edgar held up his hand like a traffic cop, and Lexi flushed.

"Well, I was just trying to explain how I knew," she said.

"That's all right, Lexi, we get the idea." Edgar glanced down the table at me. "Are you getting all this, Jessie? I guess you've heard of six degrees of separation?"

"Yes, I have. I know all about that," I told him. I nearly said that Shane had explained the expression to me, and stopped myself just in time.

Laura laughed. "See, she already knows the ropes."

Edgar looked at his watch. Laura had warned me he was a stickler for staff meetings starting and stopping on time. "That's it for today, folks. Lexi, I like your idea about the Jazz Holliday piece. If anyone can think of a way to get to her, that would be great. It sounds like it's going to have to be a personal connection, since they're keeping all this below radar at the moment. It won't do any good to go through the usual channels. You'll have to come up with something more creative." He picked up his papers. "Same time next week, folks."

When I got back to my office, I saw the message light blinking on the machine. *Shane?* I was in mood swing central, feeling the familiar buzz of excitement thinking of Shane, mixed with a feeling of crushing betrayal. What was there about Shane that brought out such strong emotions in me? Would I ever be able to relate to him without my heart shattering?

Before I could even think about listening to the message, Alicia swooped down on me. She'd been playing Freecell on her computer, but quickly minimized the screen and swiveled around in her desk chair. "So," she said with deliberate casualness, "how was the staff meeting? Did you pick up lots of inside gossip?"

I wondered how in the world she knew I had attended the staff meeting and then realized she was staring at a weekly tip sheet that Laura handed out as we left the conference room. She was squinting her eyes a little and I realized Alicia had mastered the art of reading upside down.

"It was fine," I began uncertainly. I almost said that it was a spur-of-the-moment thing and that Laura had invited me out of the blue, but stopped myself. Why should I apologize to Alicia? I didn't have to account to her for how I spent my time. She disappeared for hours without telling me and she wasn't my boss.

I was sure that Alicia was seething that she hadn't been included in the meeting, but she was acting like it was all a gigantic bore. I could tell from the way her peach-glazed nails were beating a tattoo on her Coach minibag that she wasn't quite as cool with it as she pretended to be. I stared at her, waiting, knowing there was more to come.

"Oh, by the way, Tracy was here looking for you. Apparently, you were supposed to have lunch with her." She gave me a snarky smile. *Ouch! Tracy! How could I have forgotten that?* I glanced at my watch. One forty-five. The editorial meeting had gone by in a blur and I hadn't even checked the time.

"Oh, no," I said under my breath. I reached for the phone, knowing that the faster I called and apologized, the better.

Alicia laughed, a bitter sound. "She'll live," she said shortly. "She came scurrying in here like a lost kitten left out in the rain, so I took her down to the cafeteria." She smoothed her skirt over her bony hips and stood up. "I think I'll get a chai latte, do you want anything?"

"No, thanks," I said, wishing she would leave so I could call Tracy. "And thanks for taking Tracy to the cafeteria," I said, hoping to get on her good side. "That was really nice of you."

"Oh, I'm really a nice person," Alicia sneered. "Don't believe everything you hear. Some of the people around here have nothing better to do than gossip."

The second she left, I tried to call Tracy but the line to the art department was busy. I tried a couple of more times, watching the message light blinking at me. Finally I shut my eyes and hit play. *Shane.* I knew it was him! His sexy voice drifted over the line, that incredible voice that always made my heart ping and my skin tingle. I turned down the volume in case Alicia suddenly returned with her latte. I didn't trust Alicia, and I wouldn't put it past her to spy on me. And I definitely didn't want her to know I was seeing Shane.

"Hey, darlin', just checkin' to see how things are workin' out for you. First days are always tough, but I know you can handle it. Hope you kept tonight free because you've got a date—with me!" He gave one of those low chuckles that sent my pulse racing. "I heard Edgar was driving you home tonight, but he has to stop here first to drop off something for my mom, so I told him I'd be waiting for you. We'll go out to dinner, and this time no paparazzi, I promise. I know a little place in south central L.A., they'll never find us there. See you soon, Jess!"

I pulled myself together just as Alicia came back to the office. "Is everything okay?" she said, giving me a curious stare. I could feel the color draining from my face and my legs felt wobbly. Did Shane know about the article in the gossip column linking him with Heidi? Surely he had read it—or heard about it! Or was he just playing dumb and planning on brushing the whole thing aside, as he had done before in Bedford? He had downplayed the whole incident with Heidi Hopkins, insisting that I hadn't caught them in the middle of a major clinch.

"Everything's just fine," I answered, pulling out the new employee manual Laura had given me. My thoughts were swirling, but I refused to give her the satisfaction of letting her see how rattled I was. Instead, I took a deep breath and opened the book, pretending to be absorbed in the inner workings of *Juicy.*

But I couldn't turn off the thoughts that were zipping through my brain like a pinball in an arcade machine. Should I see Shane tonight? I didn't want to call him back with Alicia sitting right there, and besides, I wasn't even sure I knew how to reach him. An out-of-area number had come up on the Caller ID, and the only other number I had for him was Lily's house. And I didn't want to put her in the middle of this, it would be too embarrassing. Why was everything with Shane so complicated?

A few minutes later, Alicia took a call, and I finally got through to Tracy down in the photo department. She seemed hurt that I had totally forgotten about our lunch date, but was willing to forgive me. "Okay, here's the deal," she said in her rapid-fire speech, "you have to tell me every tiny detail of what went on at that staff meeting, and then we'll call it square, okay?" I laughed, promised to give her all the gossip, and hung up just as Alicia turned to stare at me. She was obviously planning on eavesdropping on all my conversations, and I'd have to remember to keep my guard up.

Since I still hadn't been given any work to do, I flipped through the pages of the orientation manual, feeling Alicia's eyes rake over me. I could hardly focus on the words, though, because my thoughts zeroed in on Shane. There was nothing to do except wait until the end of the day and then confront him directly at Lily's house. It wasn't an ideal solution, but I couldn't seem to come up with a better plan.

I decided to ask him up front if he had lied about seeing Heidi Hopkins that night at the Ivy. If I wasn't satisfied with his answer, I could always insist that he drive me straight back to Ellie's. I glanced at my watch, and it seemed like the hands were frozen on two P.M. Just a few more hours until I escaped *Juicy* and found out if Shane was telling me the truth.

"SO YOU SURVIVED THE FIRST DAY AT *JUICY*, DARLIN'? I'VE BEEN thinkin' about you all afternoon, wondering if one of those sharks might have gobbled you up. I heard some of the staff members over there used to work for the tabloids and Edgar stole them away by offering them more money. You know, you gotta be careful around those guys, Jess; they eat sweet girls like you for breakfast."

I nodded, knowing why Shane felt the way he did about

entertainment reporters. My own experience at the Blue Lotus had been a real eye-opener for me. It was enough to make anyone paranoid, and as Shane liked to say, "Just because you're paranoid, doesn't mean they're not out to get you."

"I'll be careful. I promise." I had plenty of other things I wanted to talk about besides my first day at *Juicy*. I never had a chance to ask him about the Heidi Hopkins piece because he'd pulled up to Lily's house in his Jag at the exact same moment that Edgar turned into the circular driveway. I'd thanked Edgar for the ride, said good-bye to Tracy, and stepped from one car to the next. My plan to confront Shane was dead in the water. Until now.

It was six-thirty that evening, and Shane and I were sitting in a small diner in south central L.A., miles away from the celebrity hot spots in Santa Monica and the Sunset Strip.

Just as he had promised, no one was paying the slightest bit of attention to us: no crowds, no fans, no paparazzi. We were hidden away at a cozy red leather booth in the back of a tiny restaurant that was wedged between a dry cleaners and a drugstore on a side street off La Cienega. Salsa music blared from an ancient radio perched on the bright red Formica counter, and an old-fashioned ceiling fan circulated the moist air. The walls were plastered with colorful travel posters from Mexico and South America and a family with small children took up a large table in the center of the room.

When we walked in Shane greeted the owners in Spanish, and judging by the big smiles on their faces, he was obviously one of their favorite clients. I spotted his autographed head-shot hanging on the wall near the cash register.

"So tell me about your first day at *Juicy*. How did you do? Was it what you hoped it would be?" He grabbed a menu and flipped it open quickly, as if he were starving. He gave a high sign to the waiter, as if he wanted to order right away. "Sorry," he said apologetically, "I missed breakfast and lunch today."

"I think everything went okay," I said slowly. "I was invited to an editorial meeting, and I guess that's pretty unusual for a summer intern." I was staring at the menu, confused by the wide selection of Hispanic dishes, when Shane came to my rescue, doing some quick translations.

"Get the huevos rancheros," he said firmly. "That's the specialty here and hands down, they're the best in L.A. You can eat that, right?" He gave our order in rapid Spanish to the waiter, who suddenly appeared at his side.

"With iced tea, please," I added. I waited until the waiter walked away, and was steeling myself to ask about Heidi. I knew I had to do it before I lost my nerve, or I might fall under Shane's dangerous charm once again.

"Shane," I began, just as he said, "Jess," and we both laughed.

"You go first," I told him.

There was a long pause, and something flickered in those tawny dark eyes. Did he suspect that something was up? Shane leaned back in the booth, looking up idly as a young couple walked in hand in hand. For once, he wasn't sitting with his back to the door, and he'd taken his sunglasses off, so I assume he felt safe in this little neighborhood diner.

"I was going to ask you about the editorial meeting," he said lightly. "Was it very exciting, sitting there with all the reporters, hearing what kind of stories they're gonna churn out?" He was trying to act supercool, but there was something about the tenseness in his body and the wariness in his eyes that made me wonder if there was something more going on here. That it wasn't just a casual question, and that he had a stake in the answer.

For one crazy moment, I even wondered if Shane thought *he* might be the subject of a *Juicy* interview. I wondered how I'd react if his name came up at work. I knew Edgar would never permit a hatchet job on him because of his relationship with Lily, but I felt a little uneasy, just the same. I assumed Edgar would never assign me to do a story on him, because that would definitely be a conflict of interest. Edgar knew that Shane and I had done a movie together, and maybe were even an "item" as they say in the tabloids. How in the world could I ever be objective about him?

"I learned a lot about the business, just by sitting there listening," I said carefully. "How they pick celebrities for their features, what sort of stories they're looking for, and I recognized a few names being passed around. And they mentioned someone new," I said suddenly, thinking of the teen who had snared the lead in a new TV show. "A young actress who seems to be getting a lot of buzz lately, even though she's only been in Hollywood a short while."

"Really?" Shane asked lazily. "Who's that?"

"Jazz Holliday," I answered, surprised that his eyes lit up with excitement.

"You've gotta be kiddin' me. Little ole Jasmine Holliday from Fort Worth, Texas?" Shane leaned forward eagerly, resting his elbows on the table. "We did a whole series of department store commercials together when we were about eight years old. And some community theater, too. Musicals, as far as I can remember. *Oliver*, and *Annie*, and one other one. I think it was *Oklahoma!*" He laughed. "Wow, that was a long time ago. If it's the girl I'm thinking of, we went to grade school together." He paused while the waiter slid a giant platter of nachos drenched in cheese and salsa in front of us. "I had no idea she was out here in Hollywood. But come to think of it, she always talked about making the big time and getting a career in show business. How'd you happen to come across her, anyway?"

"Her name came up in reference to some new shows," I said, not wanting to give too much away. "And she calls herself Jazz, not Jasmine, if it's the same girl you're talking about."

Shane snapped his fingers. "Jazz! Yeah, that's her, all right. She took jazz and tap lessons with me back at Miss Lydia's back in Texas and she insisted we call her 'Jazz' or 'Jazzy.' That was her nickname." He laughed at the memory. "She was really something, probably five feet tall and a hundred pounds soaking wet, but that little girl could dance her heart out. She always swore she was gonna be discovered by some big talent agent someday and everyone was always teasin' her about it. Funny how things work out, isn't it?"

"Very funny," I agreed. "I guess anything can happen out here in Hollywood. You always say it's a place where dreams can come true."

Come to think of it, so much had happened to me in the last few weeks that sometimes it felt like a dream. Who would ever think that a small-town girl from Bedford would get a part in a movie, snare a really cool job in Hollywood, and date the hottest teen star in town? It sounds like something the tabloids would dream up.

"You know, I'd sure like to talk to Jazz again." He whipped out his Palm Pilot. "You don't happen to have a number for her, do you?"

I shook my head, wondering why I felt a sudden flash of jealousy. Why did it bother me that Shane wanted to reconnect with a childhood friend? *Probably because she's young, blond, and drop-dead gorgeous,* a little voice said inside me. *Another Heidi Hopkins . . .*

I sat back and shot a friendly smile at Shane. There was no point in letting him know how pathetically insecure I was! "No, I'm afraid not. I don't have any contact information on her, no number, no address," I admitted. "Someone said she's in the process of moving from a hotel to a condo, so it's hard to get in touch with her. And I don't know the name of her agent, or manager." I hesitated, wondering how much more I could safely say. I didn't dare tell him that the producers were probably keeping the new project under wraps, nixing the idea of any media coverage. Except, of course, the news releases they were putting out themselves.

"Well, I know I can track her down. I'll get Kevin on it right away. Did you want to do a story on her, or something like that?" Shane had an amazing way of cutting to the chase. How in the world had he guessed that I wanted to interview her? I wondered.

I nodded. "A story? Do we ever! But I don't even know her. Do you think she'd agree to talk to me?"

"Why wouldn't she?" Shane looked genuinely puzzled. "Actors love attention, you know that." He grinned to show he was including himself at the top of the list. "You know that old Hollywood joke. Any publicity is good publicity. Say anything you want about me, but just make sure you spell my name right." He took a gulp of iced tea and tapped his fingers on the tablecloth. As always, he was alive with energy and I could practically feel sparks flying off him. "We love to see our name in print, that's for sure."

"I hope you're right. I think she may have a solid wall of PR people between herself and the media," I said, not wanting to give too much away. "And another thing . . . I don't have a famous byline. Who am I kidding? I don't have any byline," I said with a laugh. "So she may not want to waste her time being interviewed by a nobody."

"A nobody? What in the world are you talkin' about, Jess? You're a reporter with a hot new magazine. You got nothin' to apologize for. Maybe you're not as famous as somebody like Giuliana on *E! News Live*, but hey, everyone's gotta start someplace, don't they? And *Juicy's* nothing to be ashamed about. I think it's going to be one of the top magazines once it hits the stands. Edgar's a dynamite writer and he's got big plans for it. This could be a good career move for you, you know? You could have a great future with them."

"I guess so," I said uncertainly. "If you think it's a good idea, I'll try to set up an interview with her. Assuming you can get her number, I mean." I couldn't believe I was pushing ahead with this. Just one day at *Juicy* had made me one of the "sharks" Shane had warned me about. But I had learned from that staff meeting that it was "nothing ventured, nothing gained" at *Juicy*. If you wanted something, you had to go for it full throttle, not wait for it to fall into your lap.

This was the way things were done in Hollywood. If I didn't do the story on Jazz, someone else would. And what better way to let Edgar know I was a real go-getter and an asset to his magazine than by scoring an exclusive!

"Of course I'll get her number," Shane said confidently. "And I know she'll talk to you. No problemo," he said, just as our food arrived. "I'll set everything up with her and call you back tomorrow. You can work out the details with her."

"I can't believe it's that easy."

Shane grinned at me. "It's easy because I'll talk to her, Texan to Texan. She'll come right around, you'll see. We Texans stick together." He looked up before tucking into what looked like a giant omelette. Apparently, that was the famous huevos rancheros we had ordered. He smothered it with salsa and a splash of hot sauce. "Now what was it you wanted to ask me?"

I hesitated and took a deep breath. My heart was in my throat, but this was no time to chicken out. I knew I had to put the Heidi issue to rest, once and for all. "Do you read the trades, Shane?" He looked up quizzically and I rushed on, "Because there was an item about you . . . and Heidi." I waited, and his expression didn't change. "You know," I said, as a little arrow of annoyance shot through me, "at the Ivy the other night. Together. They said you were pretty cozy together, and I think the expression they used was 'kissy-face.' " I gave an involuntary shudder and the hint of a smile touched Shane's mouth.

"Kissy-face?" he repeated slowly. "Oh that," he said, dismissively. "Kevin mentioned something about it, but I didn't bother looking at the piece myself." He shook his head, as if the whole story was made up out of thin air and not worth his time. He leaned back and gave me an appraising look. "I just knew you had somethin' on your mind tonight, Jessie, darlin'. Why didn't you just come out and ask me? We could have cleared this up in two seconds flat."

I pursed my lips. "We can still clear it up in two seconds," I pointed out. "Right here, right now. All you have to do is tell me what's going on with her."

Shane put down his fork and spread out both his hands, palms up. "There's nothin' to tell you, Jess, because nothing happened." He picked up his fork and started eating again. "At least, not the way they say. You know what these reporters do, they hang around the Ivy to see who's having dinner and to try to get a few pictures. But they need a story to go with the pictures. So what do they do? They invent something, they make it up out of the blue."

"Out of the blue?" I couldn't keep the suspicion out of my voice.

"Yeah, and they're pretty sneaky about it. Here's what they do. They put in a little tiny bit of the truth, just to make it believable, to get you hooked. But most of the story, say ninety percent, doesn't have a grain of truth in it. They do it every time," he said ruefully, "because that's how they sell papers. They fool the public by peddling gossip and pretending it's news." He stared at me, one eyebrow arched quizzically. "I'm surprised you haven't figured that out by now, just from workin' at *Juicy*. That kind of thing goes on all the time."

"But we're not talking about *Juicy*. We're talking about the piece in the *Times* about you and Heidi."

"Jessie, have you heard a word I said?" Shane's mouth started to twist in a smile, and then he noticed my chilly expression, and quickly struck a more serious pose.

"I've heard every word you said," I said tartly. "I just don't know what to make of it, that's all." My mouth was dry and I felt a lump working its way up my throat. So Shane was saying ninety percent of the story wasn't true? But what about that other ten percent? All I wanted to know is what really happened that night at the Ivy, the night he cut our date short for what he said was an important business meeting. I took a deep breath and forced myself to speak calmly, deciding there was no point in letting him know how upset I was.

"So, tell me, Shane, what part of the story isn't true? The part about Heidi being there with you, or the part about . . . you know." I couldn't bring myself to repeat the reporter's description of their make-out session because the image stabbed me like a screwdriver to the heart.

"Oh Jessie," Shane said slowly, flashing me that dangerous smile, "what am I gonna do with you? When are you gonna realize you can't believe everythin' you read?" He reached across the table and laid his hand on top of mine, sending a little surge of warmth through my body. "Heidi was there, but that's just because we happen to have the same agent. Norm figured he'd kill two birds with one stone. He'd push me for the film role, and he's been trying to get a TV deal for Heidi with the same production company." He paused while the waiter refilled our drinks. "But nothing worked out the way Norm hoped it would and it was pretty clear from the get-go that they weren't interested in Heidi. She doesn't have any dramatic reach, you know?"

Dramatic reach? She seemed to have plenty of dramatic reach when I caught her making out with Shane on the set of *Reckless Summer* just a few weeks earlier.

"I'm not talking about her acting ability, Shane," I said acidly. "I'm puzzled about something. Why would the reporter say you were doing . . . uh, what he said, if there was really nothing going on?"

Shane laughed, a throaty chuckle. "Now Jessie, you're a smart girl and I know you can tell me the answer to that one. Because it sells papers!" he said triumphantly. "That's what it's all about, making the story as over the top as you can, to sell more issues. That's the first rule at *Juicy*, I bet. You can ask Edgar if you don't believe me."

I flushed, thinking that I hadn't been a hundred percent honest with Shane about my interest in Jazz Holliday. In some ways, maybe I was no better than the reporter who had accused Shane of playing "kissy-face" with Heidi at the Ivy. After all, I had a secret agenda: I hoped to get Jazz to reveal the inside scoop on the new TV show—information that the producers were trying to keep secret. So what did that make me? Maybe I had become one of the sharks Shane had warned me about, after all!

"Now, Jessie," he said firmly, "we're not going to waste a minute of this perfect evening talking about something that never happened, are we?" His smile was so innocent, so beguiling, that I melted, letting him sweep back into my heart.

"No, I guess not." I smiled at him, feeling a rush of emotion. He was rubbing his fingers gently over the top of my hand and my heart was thumping hard against my ribs. I wanted to believe Shane, so I said exactly what he hoped I'd say. "Just forget everything I said, Shane, and let's make the most of tonight. I like having you all to myself, with no fans, no paparazzi."

Shane nodded. "I feel the same way, darlin'," he said. "I don't get many nights like this, that's for sure." He gave that sexy smile that always made my skin tingle and my heart go ping.

I grinned back at him, feeling a buzz of happiness inside. I decided to push all the doubts, suspicions, and problems out of my mind for the time being. Here I was in Hollywood, having dinner with *People* Magazine's "Sexiest Teen Alive."

I planned on enjoying every single minute of it!

Chapter Nine

★

JAZZ HOLLIDAY WAS NOTHING LIKE I HAD IMAGINED. SHE CER-
tainly wasn't five feet tall anymore, and she'd lost the braces
and freckles Shane had told me about. When I rang the bell
at her Silver Lake condo, I was surprised to see a tall, green-
eyed blonde open the door wide and usher me inside. She was
dressed in skintight white jeans, a gauzy peach-colored embroidered top, and very high sling-back heels. She must have been
five nine or ten in flats because she was well over six feet tall in
her lethal-looking stilettos. I felt like a munchkin standing next
to her.

She was drop-dead gorgeous.

"Jazz Holliday?" I asked, taken aback by her stunning good
looks. She was very slim and willowy with honey-gold hair,

river-green eyes, and Angelina Jolie lips. As far as I could tell, she wasn't wearing any makeup—a natural beauty!

"That's me, honey! C'mon in and make yourself at home."

I grinned, thinking that somehow she'd managed to keep her Texas twang in the middle of L.A. Of course, she hadn't been in town very long, I reminded myself, and I was sure that once the army of voice trainers and acting teachers and media coaches had gotten to her, she would end up with the same bland accent as everyone else on the West Coast. Shane had kept his Texas twang, but it was an integral part of his character.

Her handshake was warm and firm, and she walked ahead of me into a beautiful living room filled with Danish furniture and bright paintings splashing color on the ivory walls. It was a sophisticated look, and it made me wonder if Jazz was really the small-town girl that Shane had described to me. Someone with a real eye for color and style had done that room; it reminded me of Ellie's condo. Or did Jazz have a decorator? I'd have to ask her, I decided. It might make an interesting detail for the article, the kind of thing readers would like to know.

"I've just been dying to meet you ever since I talked to Shane," she said. She was practically gushing with emotion, but there was something about the warmth of her smile and her Dolly Parton voice that made her enthusiasm believable. Even though her condo looked like something out of *Architectural Digest*, I immediately thought this girl was the real deal, a down-home type, as Shane would say.

She curled up on a black leather sofa and played with a long Indian beaded necklace that trailed down the front of her blouse. It was one of those oversized ethnic pieces that are very hot right now. "You're my very first visitor to my new condo," she said, flashing a big smile. "I made some lemon cookies and sweet tea for us. And there's fresh mint for the tea, I grow it myself on the balcony." She pointed to a tray and glasses she had set out on the coffee table. "Help yourself."

"Thanks," I said. "That was really nice of you. I bet your fans would be surprised to know that you bake."

"Oh, I love to bake," she confided. "I've got a terrible sweet tooth. If I don't have my sugar fix every morning, I just can't function, you know? I have to make gallons of sweet tea because I drink it all day long. I put it in a big ole Mason jar and make sun tea right out on the balcony." She gave a wistful smile. "I just love sweet tea. I guess no one calls it that out here."

Sweet tea. I remembered that's what Shane called the heavily sugared drink he said reminded him of home. I thought about pulling out a steno pad to scribble a few notes, and then figured it would be better to wait a few minutes and see if Jazz would relax a little. She seemed nervous and ill at ease, talking a little too fast, twisting the glass beads round and round her fingers as if she was having trouble sitting still.

Funny, usually actresses are very good dealing with the press, and I wondered what was going through her mind. Laura had suggested asking Jazz if I could tape the interview but I had vetoed the idea. Now that I saw how tightly wound up she was, I knew a tape recorder would have been a bad idea. I was glad that I had stuck with my instincts and decided to take notes instead.

I paused, wondering how to get started. I had asked Laura for some guidelines, once Shane had given me Jazz's phone number and I knew the interview was really going to happen. Laura had told me to get enough for a short piece, maybe seven hundred fifty words, or a thousand maximum, that they could use for the next issue. If it went well, *Juicy* would send me back for a more in-depth piece later on.

"Be sure you get some good quotes," she had told me. "Something really catchy and spontaneous so we can use it in a sidebar. Ask her something out of the blue, something that will catch her off guard and shake her up a little. That's usually the best way to get a good quote. And don't just let her give you the usual PR spiel. These girls have been brainwashed to say the same thing over and over to the press. It makes for lousy copy. We need something fresh and original, but you already know that, right?"

I had nodded, pretending I knew what I was doing. Fresh and original. Laura's parting words stuck in my mind. "Don't be afraid to go for the jugular if you have to, Jess. You're not going to get a great interview by playing Ms. Nice Girl."

"This is my first Hollywood interview," Jazz said, her soft voice cutting into my thoughts. She poured herself a glass of tea and took a big gulp, as if she wanted something solid to hold onto.

Mine, too, I nearly said. Instead, I shot her a reassuring look. "I thought you'd be an old hand at this. Shane tells me you were practically a child star when the two of you caught the acting bug back in Texas."

She waved her hand dismissively. "Oh, that was just amateur stuff, you know, recitals at the local dancing school and community theater stuff. You know how Shane always puts a good spin on things. He's a sweetheart, but he's got a real vivid imagination, if you know what I mean."

Do I ever! I thought.

She smiled disarmingly. "Guess it's the actor in him. He can't help it, you know, but that boy loves to exaggerate." A soft breeze drifted in from the balcony, riffling the gauzy curtains. "Oh, would you like to sit outside? I do some of my best thinking out there. I've got the world's smallest balcony," she said with a giggle. "It's the size of a postage stamp. There's just enough room for two chairs and a tiny table."

"We can sit wherever you're the most comfortable," I told her.

She started to get up and then sat down quickly. "Oh, wait," she said, frowning. "On second thought, it's real sunny out there, so maybe we better stay inside. I'm not supposed to get a tan, not even a little bit. They want me to be really pale—" She broke off abruptly as if she had said too much.

"Why shouldn't you get a tan?" I said casually. "I thought fake-bakes were really popular out here. Paris Hilton started the whole trend when she talked about Mystic Tans in her new book, didn't she?" Jazz had a stricken look on her face, and I remembered someone at *Juicy* saying that *Bad Intentions*, the new TV show, was supposed to take place in Chicago in the dead of winter. No wonder they told Jazz not to get a tan!

The question obviously threw her, because she started chewing on a polished fingernail and a frown line appeared between her perfectly arched eyebrows. "Um," she said, licking her lips, "well, you know, they say the sun is really bad for your skin. You know, lines and freckles and all that." Jazz was a terrible liar, the worst I've ever seen.

"I've heard that, too," I agreed, wondering where the conversation was headed. I tried to sound relaxed and friendly, hoping she didn't realize I wasn't buying her clumsy cover-up. Since I'm a terrible liar myself, I knew how frantic she must be feeling right now.

"And the pale look is in right now," she added. "Just think of Marcia Cross on *Desperate Housewives*. I just love her porcelain complexion, don't you? You can tell she doesn't spend a single second in the sun!" She thought she'd made a quick recovery, but I wasn't fooled for a minute. I would have to play this carefully, because I could see that her guard was up.

I nodded, thinking I better get some of this down in my notes. As casually as I could, I pulled out my notebook, ignoring the look of alarm on Jazz's face. "You don't mind if I make a few notes while we talk, do you? It'll help me be more accurate when I sit down to the write the article." Laura had come up with that line, warning me that people often felt uncomfortable if you pulled out a notebook, so it was a good idea to reassure them ahead of time.

"No, of course not," she said quickly. "That's fine." She blinked twice, and I knew she was regretting her remark about the sun. "So, do you want to hear all about Texas?" she said hopefully. "How I got interested in acting and where I went to school?"

"Sure," I said, sitting back. "Tell me about your early days onstage and what it was like to do all those commercials and the little theater productions. It must have been very exciting for you."

"Oh, it was!" she said girlishly, her face lighting up. "My whole family turned out for every single play . . ."

I let Jazz ramble on for the next half hour about her Fort Worth experiences, her friends, her family, her pets, knowing none of it would make it into print. But it was important to get her warmed up, to gain her trust, and then I could move into the area that Laura had called "fresh and original." Meaning, her top-secret starring role in *Bad Intentions.*

I had been there for nearly an hour when the phone rang in the kitchen. Jazz looked at the clock and jumped up in alarm, nearly spilling her glass of sweet tea. "Oh, my gosh, that's my momma calling from Texas," she exclaimed. "Do you mind if I take it? I promise I'll only be a minute. I completely forgot I promised to call her this afternoon."

"Go ahead," I said, settling back into the cushions. "Take your time, I'll go over my notes."

When Jazz left the room, I idly looked over the pile of magazines stacked neatly under the coffee table. *InStyle, Jane, Elle, People,* and *In Touch.* Jazz obviously liked fashion and celebrity gossip, I decided. It was exciting to think that in a couple of weeks, a brand new issue of *Juicy* would be there, and one of the pieces would have my byline! Would Jazz like the article? That depends on what I say, I thought ruefully. And the main question should be: Will Edgar like the article?

I was thumbing through an issue of *Lucky,* checking out some cool camis, when something under the coffee table caught my eye. I spotted a piece of sky-blue construction paper tucked under the bottom of the pile of magazines. Just the corner was showing, as if someone had shoved it in there hurriedly, wanting to get it out of sight.

Curious, I tugged at it, and pulled out what looked like a television script! A bright blue cardboard cover, front and back, held together with three brass-colored brads. The title page read: *Bad Intentions. Episode One. "Tricia Goes for the Gold." by Jim West and Roger Herschfield.* I had never heard of the writers, but now that I had their names, I could Google them.

I glanced nervously toward the kitchen were Jazz was still yakking away with her mom. I couldn't believe my luck! I quickly thumbed through the script. Someone had highlighted all of Tricia's dialogue, and had put in marks for the "beats," like method actors do.

Shane had explained the technique to me when we were acting together in *Reckless Summer* back in Bedford. He told me that actors put a vertical line between sections of dialogue, called "beats," and that it helps them memorize the script and get a handle on their role.

In this episode, it looked like the main character, Tricia, was training for some sort of competition, maybe a marathon race? The race was going to be held in Chicago in the dead of winter, and the prize was a full scholarship to the college of her choice. The other characters, including Tricia's family and boyfriend, seemed to be against the idea, and were trying to discourage her. But why? I couldn't figure it out but I flipped through the pages as quickly as I could, trying to get a sense of the characters and plot.

I was deep in the dialogue when I suddenly realized Jazz was wrapping up her phone conversation and would be back in the living room any second. Just in time, I shoved the script back under the pile of magazines, and pretended to be scanning my notes as she appeared in the doorway.

Now I knew my hunch was right—Jazz really had landed the part of Tricia, the lead in *Bad Intentions*! But could I get her to admit it? And what was the best way to handle it? I decided not to let her know I was snooping, and would give her a chance to tell me about it herself.

"Sorry about that," she said a little uncertainly. Her eyes strayed to the pile of magazines under the table, and I wondered if she was regretting taking the call.

"It's no problem," I said, smiling. "My mom checks in with me, too."

"Well, sometimes it's a little embarrassing. I mean, I know she's worried and all, but I'm really old enough to live on my own, you know? Some of my friends from back home are even married! But my mom just can't believe I'm grown up, and she still worries that I'm not eating enough." She stopped suddenly, a panicky look in her eyes. "Oh," she said in a strangled voice, "you're not going to print all that, are you? My mom would be really hurt. And I didn't mean it the way it sounded . . ." She gave me an imploring look and I shook my head.

"Don't worry. That's not the kind of thing I would ever print." I gave her my brightest smile. "I have a mom, too, you know. And she worries about me all the time." I knew I couldn't get sidetracked on a discussion of our mothers, and I had to steer the conversation back to *Bad Intentions*. I wondered how far I could push Jazz.

"What else would you like to know?" she asked, looking relieved.

"Well, I'd like to know about your television plans," I said casually. "I hear you're up for the lead in *Bad Intentions*." I was supercool when I said this, pretending it was no big deal, but Jazz acted like I had detonated a hand grenade in her living room.

"You know about that?" she blurted out, and then clapped her hand over her mouth. "I didn't think anybody knew about the show! They said they want to keep it quiet for the time being." Her hand went to her throat and she shook her head in disbelief.

"Really?" I struggled to look surprised. "But Jazz, everyone knows about the show and that you got the lead. Hey, it's really good news, you should be proud of it. Congratulations."

"Well, thanks, I guess," she said, sitting down slowly. "I just didn't know they were going public with it yet. This is all news to me."

"Why wouldn't they go public with it?" I asked innocently. "It's probably going to be the hottest new show on the fall lineup. Gosh, Jazz, you know what that means! You're gonna be a major star. I thought you'd be doing tons of interviews by now."

"No, I haven't done any," she said slowly. "I've just been holed up here, all alone, studying my script. I haven't had any company since I moved here."

"I bet you will be, very soon," I told her. "Before you know it, *Access Hollywood* will be beating down your door."

Jazz gave a shy smile, suddenly looking younger than her eighteen years. "I don't think that's gonna happen anytime soon," she said quickly. "Nobody's asking for interviews, because I haven't told a soul about the show. They made me promise, you know," she added, her green eyes serious.

"They?"

"The producers. I'm not sure, but I think it's even written in my contract somewhere. I never even read the whole thing,

I just let my agent handle it. But if you know about my getting the lead, I guess it must be okay." She relaxed and hugged a throw pillow to her chest. "How did you find out about my getting the part, anyway? I haven't seen anything about it in any of the trades." She glanced down at the coffee table.

I thought it was interesting that she still wasn't willing to show me the script she had tucked away there.

"Well, it's my business to know," I hedged. "That's what entertainment reporters do. We have a lot of contacts in the business and we like to be on the cutting edge." I grinned. "At least, that's what we try to do."

Jazz laughed. "Of course you do. Honestly, Jess, you must think I'm a total idiot. It's just that I'm so new at this."

"I think you'll catch on fast," I said truthfully. "I've only been here a few days, and I'm getting an idea of how things are done. You pick it up as you go along."

"Really?" She picked at a thread on the embroidered throw pillow. "I guess I should pay more attention to the business end of things. I've just been kind of going with the flow, letting other people tell me what to do."

"That would probably be a good idea," I agreed. My heart sank when I looked at Jazz. She was way too trusting to survive in Hollywood, and I caught myself wondering what the fallout from this interview would be for her. The interview was a huge success for me, but what would it mean for her?

"You know, when Shane asked if I'd give you an interview, I tried to clear it with my publicist but I never got through to her. She's down in Palm Springs for some celebrity golf tournament for the weekend." She glanced at her watch. "She's not coming back until really late tonight, so I guess I'll have to call her in the morning. I bet she'll really be surprised," she added, looking pleased. "She'll be impressed when she finds out I was interviewed for a new magazine."

So the publicist was away for the weekend! What a lucky break for *Juicy*, and for me, I thought. "Tell me a little about the audition. Did you know the people you were reading for? Did they come to Texas or did you fly out here?"

"It was one of those once-in-a-lifetime weird things," Jazz said, warming up to the topic. "My best friend knows the assistant director on a Fox show, and he mentioned that they were going to be casting this really funny family comedy set in Chicago. And Marcy, that's my friend, told him I would be just perfect for the lead. I can't believe that girl!" she gushed. "But sure enough, he called me one night and asked me to send him a headshot. And the next thing you know, I was on a plane for Los Angeles. They put me up in this really nice hotel, the Beverly Wilshire, and everybody was so friendly. I wasn't the least bit nervous when I had to read for them."

I let Jazz talk about the "friendly folks" she met in Hollywood, how she felt the part was written for her, how much she liked the actors she read with, and so on. Jazz painted a golden glow over the whole audition process, but she seemed like such a genuinely sweet girl that I suppose she saw everything like that. She clearly had no idea what a dog-eat-dog world she was in.

The sun was setting when I finally stood up and closed my notebook. I had tons of material, more than I could ever use for a short article, and I hoped Laura would keep her word and assign me to a more in-depth piece later on.

Jazz hesitated at the door, as if she was struggling with something, "Um, you think this is going to be okay, don't you?" She ran her hand through her long golden hair and looked at me uncertainly. "About the interview, I mean?"

"Sure, why wouldn't it be?" I gave her my most reassuring smile. This was no time for doubts; I already had the interview and it would be hitting the stands in a couple of weeks.

"I don't know," she said, "I was just thinking that maybe I should have waited until I cleared it with Renee, my publicist." She waited for me to say something, and when I was silent, she went on. "But Shane said you were going to be over this way today, and it would be good to get it out of the way. And he said the publicity in the first issue of *Juicy* would really be good for me and for my career."

"Well, as usual, Shane is right," I told her. "We'll send over the photographer to take some nice pictures to go with the article. He's a genius, I know you'll like him."

"Oh, I just know I will, too!" she said. And then, to my surprise, she leaned over and gave me a big hug. "You've been so nice, Jessie, I just can't believe I made a new friend this soon. I hope we can get together again real soon and maybe go out for lunch or coffee. We have so much in common, both of us being new in town, and all."

I tried not to groan. A friend? I thought how Alicia, my office mate, would hoot if she knew Jazz felt that way. Shane always said that rule number one in Hollywood is: *Reporters are not your friends.* And rule number two? *Never forget rule number one.*

"SO YOU GOT EVERYTHING YOU HOPED FOR?" IT WAS EARLY THE next morning, and Laura stuck her head in my office to see how the Jazz interview had gone. Alicia had just strolled in, nearly half an hour late, and was pretending to check her e-mail. I didn't have to look around to know she was hanging on my every word.

"I got more than I hoped for," I said. "There's a lot of material there." I wondered how much to use in the story, and was just about to ask Laura for advice when she glanced at her watch and rearranged her papers.

"I've got a budget meeting with Edgar," she said, "but here's what I'd like you to do." She paused, thinking. "Write up a thousand words for me, and get it on my desk by next week." She must have seen my look of alarm, because she laughed. "Just a rough draft, Jessie, not the finished product. I want to see what you've got and where you're heading with it. It'll take me less time to offer some editorial input that way. Just hit the high points, the really good stuff. We can flesh it out later."

"Sure, that's fine. I'll get on it right away," I promised.

"And you can call me if you have any questions," she added. "I'll be in my office all afternoon." And with that she disappeared.

"Sounds like you scored a major hit," Alicia sneered. "So what did Jazz tell you? Did she admit that the whole star search thing was a giant hoax?"

I sat down, swiveling to face my computer. Alicia was starting to annoy me, and the idea of spending the whole summer with her was seeming less and less appealing. "We didn't get into that aspect of it, really." I stared at the screen and opened a blank file, hoping she would get the hint and start her own work. Alicia, being Alicia, ignored the hint completely.

"You mean she didn't admit she already had the starring role? I thought that was the whole idea behind the piece!"

"That's part of it," I said, turning to look at her directly. "But it's not the whole thing. I'm doing more of a human-interest piece, what it's like to be a new actress in Hollywood. She's a small-town girl from Texas and all this is new to her."

Alicia snorted. "She can't be as small-town as you think if she's dating Shane Rockett."

"She's not dating Shane Rockett!" I blurted out without thinking. From the smile on Alicia's face, I knew that was a test question. She was on a fishing expedition and I had walked right into her trap! "They're friends, that's all. They knew each other back in Texas when they were little kids."

"How sweet," Alicia said sarcastically. "Do you really think that's the kind of material *Juicy* wants in the feature? Here's a news flash, Jess. They don't want a human-interest piece, they want a hatchet job. And if you can't produce one, they'll send back another reporter who can." It was clear from Alicia's self-satisfied expression that she was talking about herself.

"It's nice of you to be so concerned with the article, Alicia," I said, smiling sweetly, "but I know exactly how to slant it. Thanks for your input, though." And with that, I swiveled back to my computer and turned my back on Alicia.

By midmorning, I was deep into a profile of Jazz, trying to capture her sweetness, her beauty, her Texas charm. I was alone in the office, writing quickly, hoping to turn out a quick draft by lunchtime. When the phone rang, I picked it up without taking my eyes off the screen, not wanting to break the flow.

"Editorial," I said softly, tucking the receiver under my ear so I could keep on typing.

There was dead silence, then a teary voice. "Jessie, is that you? Shane gave me your number."

I glanced at the Caller ID. Jazz! Something was very wrong, and I could make a quick guess—the publicist had probably returned from Palm Springs and gone ballistic when she heard about my visit.

"Jazz," I said pleasantly, "how's it going?" My fingers continued to fly over the keys.

"Oh, Jessie, I've made a terrible mistake," she wailed. "Just terrible. I've made an awful mess of things and I don't know what to do. You've got to help me!" This was followed by a series of snuffling noises that sounded like sobs.

"Jazz, calm down, I can't understand you," I said. "What's wrong?"

"Everything!" she gasped, and this brought on a new wave of tears. "I never should have agreed to the interview with you. Renee is furious with me. She'll probably call you later today, but I thought I should talk to you first. She's not very nice when she's mad."

I smiled. "I think I can handle Renee," I said smoothly. "But what exactly is the problem?"

"The show, it's the show!" Jazz insisted. "I never should have mentioned it. Jess, if you print that part about me getting the lead, it could ruin everything! They might take me off the show. They can do it, you know. They can say that I broke the agreement. My agent, Sheila, told me that. She's mad at me, too," Jazz said miserably.

I sighed. I never thought things would get to this point. Getting a good story was one thing, but causing Jazz to lose her acting job was another. If she lost the role on *Bad Intentions*, she'd probably end up back in Fort Worth.

"Are you still there?" Jazz said, sniffing a little.

"I'm here." I looked at the screen, wondering how much of a piece I had without the *Bad Intentions* bombshell. Not very much.

"Jess, I'm begging you! You can't print that article!" She hesitated. "You haven't turned it in yet, have you?"

"No, I haven't," I admitted. "I'm just in the middle of writing it up. I need to turn in something by next week. They want to see a first draft, so they can see what direction I'm going in with the story."

"Then it's not too late!" Jazz said gratefully. "You can still change it around, can't you?" I didn't answer, and she hurried on, "Look, Jessie, do you want to come back for another interview? I'll make sure you get enough for a nice article. I'll give you loads of information about myself."

"I need a few minutes to figure out what to do," I admitted. "I'm not sure how to handle this." My mind was racing, flipping through the choices I could make and the possible outcomes of those choices. I stared at the screen, realizing my story was falling apart before my eyes. One phone call had changed everything. And who could I ask for advice? I knew what Laura's answer would be.

What would happen if I didn't mention that Jazz had gotten the lead in *Bad Intentions*? That was the whole focus of the article. Without it, there wasn't any hook, and it would just be another ho-hum celeb profile. Laura would wonder what happened, and someone else might be reassigned to the story. It would certainly hurt my internship at *Juicy*. But there was even more at stake for Jazz—what would happen to her career if I printed it?

"Jess, please tell me you're not going through with this! Please, say something! Tell me what you're thinking."

I'm thinking I'm losing the biggest scoop of my life, I wanted to say. "I don't need to do another interview, Jazz," I said, finally. "I already have lots of material. I could slant the piece toward your life in L.A. and what it's like for a small-town girl to move to Hollywood. They call it a fish-out-of-water story. Maybe something like that would work." I breathed out a sigh. My dreams of writing a really spectacular cover story were crushed, but what else could I do? Jazz was counting on me, and the vulnerability in her voice tugged at my heart. I knew exactly how she felt: frightened, worried, afraid she had wrecked her career before it had even started. Why could I tune in to her fears so perfectly? Because I was feeling the same way myself! My career at *Juicy* was up for grabs if I decided to kill the exclusive on Jazz and *Bad Intentions*.

"And you won't say anything about *Bad Intentions*? You promise?"

I gulped. I knew I had to do the right thing. And I had to do it now. "Not a word, Jazz. You can count on that."

"Oh, thank you, thank you, Jessie, you're the best!" she said, half-crying with relief. "I just knew I could straighten things out if I talked to you. I'll tell Sheila and Renee, and then you won't have to be bothered with them calling you."

"That would be nice," I admitted. "But Jazz, let me ask you something."

"Anything."

"When it's time to go public with the *Bad Intentions* news, you'll let *Juicy* be the first to know, won't you?"

"I'll be on the phone to you in two seconds flat, Jess. You have my word on it. You can have an exclusive, if you want!"

"Okay then," I said, smiling in spite of myself. Maybe I didn't really have a killer instinct after all, because I knew I could never do anything to ruin Jazz's career. "Gotta get back to work. I'll call you soon, Jazz."

"And we'll go out to lunch or have coffee, and have some serious girl talk!"

Chapter Ten

★

I WAS JUST RECOVERING FROM MY CONVERSATION WITH JAZZ when Alicia slipped into the office, a sly smile curling her lips. She was reading a tabloid newspaper with rapt absorption; eyes widened, brows arched, an expression of jaw-dropping surprise on her face. It reminded me of an exercise from Acting 101: "Enter stage right, reading a newspaper. Register a look of shocked surprise. No dialogue is necessary. Your facial expression and body language should convey the complexity of your inner emotional state to the audience." Hmm. Nice try, except Alicia was a terrible actress and was about as convincing as Madonna playing Mother Teresa.

When she saw that I wasn't going to react to her little improv, she finally locked eyes with me and said flatly, "Wow, was

I ever wrong about Shane Rockett and Jazz Holliday. Looks like he's not dating her after all. He's back with Blondie. I guess all the gossip was true, after all."

"Blondie?" The word leaped out before I could stop myself.

"Heidi Hopkins," she said. Her smile was calculatingly sincere, but her voice throbbed with venom. "Funny, isn't it?"

"I don't know," I said carefully. "They've known each other for a long time. They acted together in *Reckless Summer*." Alicia had been gunning for me ever since Laura invited me to the staff meeting that very first day. I could feel waves of jealousy emanating from her, like steam rising from a highway on a hot summer day.

"Oh, it's way more than that!" Alicia hooted. "Seems like they were hitting the club scene last night. Here, read it for yourself. I've got a ton of work to do." She gave an exhausted sigh and fell back into her desk chair, but not before shooting me a long, hard look. "Maybe we should do a feature on Shane and his string of girlfriends," she purred. "I bet he's got the biggest black book in Hollywood. Now *that* would make for some interesting reading! I think I'll run that idea by Laura the next time I see her."

I sighed and scanned the article. It was Shane all right, and it looked like he was holding Heidi by the elbow, steering her into a hot nightclub in Puerto Vallarta. "They're Back Together Again, and This Time It's For Keeps!" the headline screamed.

I read the first paragraph, and my heart felt like someone had slammed my chest with a sledgehammer. I knew Alicia was watching me, so I put the paper facedown on my desk, blinking fast to hide the hot tears that had sprung to my eyes. "Alicia," I said in my best I-could-care-less voice, "can you catch the phones for a minute? I want to run down to the cafeteria to get some iced tea."

"Sure." She shot me a puzzled frown as her phone rang, wondering why I hadn't collapsed in a soggy heap on the office floor.

I took the opportunity to scoot out the door and take a deep, steadying breath as I raced to the elevator. My heart felt like it was ripped to shreds, but I reminded myself that this was no time to fall apart—I had a story to write! If Shane was playing kissy-face, or lip-locking, or whatever they called it in Hollywood, with the gorgeous Heidi Hopkins, there was nothing I could do about it. At least that's what I tried to tell myself.

I dashed onto the elevator just as the doors started to close and found myself face-to-face with Edgar Harrison. "Jessie, my dear," he said heartily. "Perfect timing. I've got a surprise for you, something that I think will make you very happy." He leaned in toward me and lowered his voice as if he was about to share a wonderful secret. "How'd you like to cover the Teen Choice Awards for us?"

"The Teen Choice Awards?" I said blankly. I couldn't even process what he was saying because my mind was still swirling with the Jazz Holliday article and the "back together again" bombshell about Shane and Heidi. Talk about information overload!

Edgar's face fell and his mouth twitched in annoyance. "Surely you've heard of them, Jessie. An annual event? Honoring the top teen entertainers in Hollywood? Covered by media all over the world?" There was a not-so-gentle reprimand in his eyes and a chilly tone crept into his carefully modulated voice. He was probably wondering how he could have hired someone so hopelessly out of touch with popular culture that she hadn't heard of the Teen Choice Awards, one of the biggest events in Hollywood!

"Oh yes," I babbled. "Of course I've heard of them, Edgar. I'm just surprised, that's all. I know it's one of the biggest nights in Hollywood, and I figured you'd choose one of your regular entertainment reporters to cover it. Not a lowly summer intern like me." I smiled to show I was teasing him a little.

Edgar looked visibly relieved and took a sip of his Starbucks coffee. "That's very modest of you, Jessie, but you're not just any summer intern, you know. I heard from Laura that you snared an exclusive with Jazz Holliday for us. I'm looking forward to seeing it in print. Good work gets rewarded here at *Juicy*." He paused. "I predict great things for you here."

"I appreciate your confidence in me, I really do." I stared into Edgar's icy green eyes and nearly confessed that the Jazz Holliday story wasn't turning out the way I had planned, but the words stuck in my throat. My heart was thumping with excitement at my new assignment and I just couldn't ruin the magic of the moment. "I never expected anything like this," I said honestly.

"Well, this is what I have in mind for you. You'll be covering a large part of the ceremony, doing standup at the red carpet interviews, catching the stars as they come in, and then attending some of the parties afterward. There's one at Spago that I definitely want you to go to. It's strictly A-list and you'll get some of your best interviews there. Laura will go over the details with you, and she'll give you a couple of tickets for the Spago party. You can take your friend Tracy if you like."

"Spago!" I exclaimed. "I'd love to!" I had heard about the famous restaurant overlooking the Sunset Strip. It was a popular star hangout, with a superfamous owner (Wolfgang Puck), a six-month waiting list, and veggie pizza to die for.

"I thought you'd like the idea," Edgar said. I must have redeemed myself with my enthusiasm, because he smiled at me, his eyes twinkling. "Oh, one more thing. I decided to send Alicia along with you. It wouldn't do to show any favoritism, and after all, she's covering teen celebrities for us, too. Plus the two of you work together, and *Juicy* is all about team players."

"Of course," I agreed, my spirits sinking. Alicia? Just what I needed to ruin my big night! "I think she'll be really excited to go." *Team players*. I had heard that expression since the day I started at *Juicy*.

"And I suppose you know who's hosting the awards this year?" Edgar said. "It's been all over the trades."

"Um, actually, I don't know." Edgar raised his eyebrows, and I could feel my face flush with embarrassment. So much had happened so quickly that I hadn't even had time to read the press releases that had crossed my desk on the awards presentation.

"Someone we're both fond of," Edgar said, as the bell pinged and the doors opened on the bottom floor. He waited until we stepped out to drop the bomb. "Your good friend, Shane Rockett."

"I CAN'T BELIEVE YOU'RE COVERING THE TEEN CHOICE AWARDS!" Tracy was beside herself with excitement. The sun was setting over the Pacific in a tangerine blaze and we decided to have a late dinner on Ellie's balcony that evening. We had the place to ourselves, since Ellie was working late in town, setting up paintings for a one-woman show the following week. It was a perfect southern California evening, soft and balmy, and I tilted my head back, taking a deep breath of the salty ocean air.

"Correction, *we're* covering them," I told her. "We're a team, remember? Just part of one big, happy family."

Tracy grinned. "Oh yeah," she said laughing. "One big happy family! That's right out of the *Juicy* new employee handbook. Chapter Three. You and Your Co-Workers, Teammates, and Friends." She helped herself to another slice of mushroom-and-green-pepper pizza, catching a stray strand of runny cheese with the corner of her napkin. "Speaking of co-workers, how are things going with Alicia? You didn't say anything about her on the way home tonight." Edgar had given us a ride home again, so of course we had kept the conversation on neutral topics.

I quickly filled her in on Alicia's latest snarky behavior, and the way she'd gloated over the Shane–Heidi article in the tabloids.

Tracy listened carefully, her eyes serious. "Wow, that must have seemed like a shocker when you read it, but I'm glad you kept your cool." She hesitated. "Shane back with Heidi—again? I don't buy it. Just because they print something, doesn't mean it's true. We both know that from the press coverage on *Reckless Summer.*"

I knew it took a lot for Tracy to admit that, because she'd never trusted Shane back in Bedford and knew about his reputation with starlets. But she also knew about the tabloids and their eagerness to print anything to get a good story. "So what's the next step?" she said, cutting into my thoughts. "Have you asked him about it?"

"No, I feel like I've been down this road before." I let a soft sigh escape. "I haven't said a word to Shane because I haven't heard from him. He's down in Mexico City scouting out some film locations, so we'll be out of touch for a few more days. In fact, I probably won't see him until the night of the awards."

"Won't that seem strange? Waiting for him on the red carpet, with a mike in hand?"

"A little, I guess. Since he's hosting them, I may not run into him until after the whole thing is over. Laura's supposed to explain what I need to do, but I think what they really want is a piece on who's wearing what, and who designed it. She never got back to me, so I'll have to play it by ear. But I think it's more of a fashion piece, really." I stared down at the boardwalk and the famous Santa Monica Pier, with its passing parade of beautiful girls on inline skates and buff guys sporting muscle T-shirts. "I haven't even had time to think about what's going on with Shane. The thing I'm really worried about is the Jazz Holliday piece," I said. "There's no easy way out of this one, I'm afraid. Either way, someone's going to be very disappointed."

Tracy nodded sympathetically. I had already laid out the options for her. "But you've already made up your mind what you're going to do, haven't you?" She gave me a small, rueful smile. "You're not going to say anything about *Bad Intentions*, are you?"

I nodded. "Not a word. I promised Jazz I wouldn't." I was silent for a moment. "So the only thing left to do now is tell Laura, and I'm not looking forward to it. I feel like delaying it as long as possible."

"Maybe you should wait and tell her after the awards?"

"I'm tempted, but I'm not sure what I'll do. I think I'll just have to play it by ear."

"JUST THE PERSON I'VE BEEN LOOKING FOR!" LAURA SAID, PASS-ing me in the hallway the next morning. She was doing a delicate balancing act, holding a pile of folders in one hand and a cup of steaming coffee in the other. "We need to go over some details about the Teen Choice Awards. I heard Edgar gave you the job of covering them." She shifted her weight from one foot to the other as if her trendy stiletto heels were killing her. "It's a plum assignment, you'll love it."

"I think you had something to do with that, thanks," I said. "I appreciate the vote of confidence."

"You don't need to thank me, you earned it," she said quickly, waving a hand dismissively in the air. "It's not a favor, really. Edgar wanted the best person for the job and I put in a word for you, that's all. Do you have something to wear to the awards?"

Something to wear? I shook my head. Figuring out what to wear that night was the last thing on my mind! I had a zillion other more pressing problems weighing me down. "Not yet," I said slowly. "I haven't had a chance to think about it. I'll have to go shopping, I guess. I didn't bring many dressy clothes with me."

"Well, that's a good reason to hit the stores," she said cheerfully. "Buy something fabulous and charge it to *Juicy*. Just save the receipt and I'll make sure it goes through Accounting."

"Wow, you can do that?" I was impressed in spite of myself.

"Of course. You're representing *Juicy* at the event," she reminded me, "and we want you to look your best. Plus the on-air talent usually ends up in a lot of the shots, so people all over the country will be watching you. I have a personal shopper who can help you. I'll ask her to give you a call and you can set up an appointment. In fact, if you just give her your size, she'll send over half a dozen dresses, and you can pick out whichever one you want. That's probably the quickest way to do it." She smiled.

"Don't feel you have to hold back. After all, this is your big night, too. Your first time interviewing stars on the red carpet."

"Laura, there's something I need to tell you—" I began.

"Sorry, but it'll have to wait, Jess. I'm late already." She smiled apologetically. "I'll e-mail you with some suggestions about who to interview that night, okay? Sometimes it's a real jungle at these awards, with all the reporters jockeying for position."

"But I'd hoped we could talk," I cut in. "Just for a few minutes."

"Oh Jess," she said, rolling her eyes, "this week is totally crazy! And I'm going to New York for a few days midweek, so I don't really know when I'd have the time to meet one-on-one. But we can e-mail back and forth. It really works better for me that way. You don't mind, do you?"

"No, of course not." It didn't really matter whether I minded or not because she had already flashed me a wide grin and disappeared down the corridor, clattering away on her towering heels.

"What was that all about?" Alicia had sidled up behind me silently and was staring after Laura, her eyes flashing with curiosity.

"Nothing," I said briskly, "just going over a few details for the Teen Choice Awards."

"It looks like we're covering it together," Alicia said, giving me a hint of a smile. Maybe she was taking this team player thing more seriously than I had realized. "Of course, you'll probably get the best interviews," she added nastily. "You'll be talking to the stars, the really hot actors, and I'll be stuck with the has-beens and losers. You know, the leftovers."

"Alicia, what are you talking about?" I said, turning to walk back to my office. "We're both assigned to do red carpet interviews. I don't have any seniority over you; in fact, you were at *Juicy* first. I'm sure Laura is going to divide things up equally."

"Equally?" She snorted. "I don't think so. After all, we're not exactly equal, are we? There's the Shane Rockett connection," she said slyly. "You have it, and I don't. That's a pretty big difference, I'd say."

"I don't know what you're talking about," I said, the blood rushing to my cheeks. "Shane's hosting the awards, and that's all. If you're reading something else into it, it's just not true."

Alicia gave a bark of laughter, a short, gravelly sound that was at odds with her delicate features and innocent blue eyes. "Look, Jess, the word around here is that you and Shane are seeing each other, so don't play dumb with me. It's not what you know, it's who you know out here. If you haven't figured that out by now, you're pathetic." And with that, she turned on her heel and flounced away, her Miu Miu pleated skirt swishing softly against her tanned legs.

THE NEXT FEW DAYS PASSED QUICKLY, AND I FINALLY SAT DOWN one evening to call Marc, my on-again, off-again boyfriend down in New Orleans. I'd put off contacting Marc for the last couple of weeks, because I knew it was going to be a difficult conversation. I was confused about my feelings for him, and things were still up in the air with Shane.

Part of the problem was that I honestly didn't know where my relationship with Shane was headed. I hadn't heard a word from him since he'd left town to scout shooting locations in Mexico for his next movie. Shane isn't the kind of guy who would think to make a romantic late-night phone call or even send a funny postcard when he's off somewhere on business. It would never occur to him. He's completely obsessed with acting, and I realized that after working on *Reckless Summer* with him back in Bedford. Career always comes first with Shane, and anyone who wants to be part of his world has to accept that. As I told Tracy, I may have to accept it, but that doesn't mean I have to like it!

"Jessie!"

A wave of guilt washed over me when Marc's voice, warm and sexy, raced over the line. He sounded like he was glad to hear from me, happily forgetting the fact that I had ignored him since I'd gone out to Hollywood. Marc is a one-in-a-million guy, as Tracy never fails to remind me.

"Jess, you're famous!" he said. "I saw a picture of you standing outside a nightclub in Los Angeles. It ran in the entertainment section of the *Times-Picayune*. My mom framed it and hung it up by the cash register."

Aargh. The picture taken in front of the Blue Lotus. I should have known that shot would come back to haunt me. Funny, he didn't mention seeing Shane standing next to me; maybe he figured it was better to ignore that part of the picture.

"It was business, just business," I said quickly. "I write celebrity pieces now for a new magazine called *Juicy*. It hits the stands next week, the day of the Teen Choice Awards." I took a deep breath and quickly filled him in on everything that had happened to me since I'd flown out to Los Angeles from Bedford.

"You look so beautiful in the picture," he said softly when I finished. There was silence on the line and then he said in a husky voice, "I really miss you, Jess. When are you coming down here for a visit?"

I felt a pang go through me at the yearning in his voice. If I hadn't met Shane, Marc LaPierre would be the best thing that ever happened to me. Tall, handsome, incredibly sexy, and a genuinely nice guy. Plus smart, funny, and crazy in love with me! As Tracy always says about Marc, what's not to like?

"I don't know when I'll ever have time to fly down to Louisiana," I said honestly. "Things are really jammed out here." I winced. I was beginning to sound just like Laura. Busy, busy. "The new job is such a great opportunity, and it looks like I'll be staying out here for the summer." I let my voice trail off, wondering how to explain the whirlwind that was my life in Hollywood. Marc had spent his whole life in New Orleans, growing up with the same friends, helping out at his parents' bed and breakfast, playing drums in the school marching band, and going to jazz concerts in Old Town. Hollywood was so far out of his experience, it was like trying to describe life on another planet.

Marc had the kind of life I used to have back in Bedford, come to think of it. A nice, ordinary quiet life that was fun, but had no surprises, no excitement. *No magic?* I caught myself thinking. Hollywood had changed me already.

We talked for a few more minutes, mostly about how business had picked up at The Black Swan, his family's bed and breakfast, and some of the improvements they'd made to the property. We both carefully avoided talking about the possibility of him flying out to the West Coast. I knew all I had to do was say the word, and Marc would be on the next plane to LAX. But that was the last thing I wanted. My life was complicated enough.

I was wondering how to wrap up the conversation when Marc was suddenly called away to help out in the kitchen. "Jessie, I've gotta run," he said breathlessly. "We have a new chef, and I thinking he's doing his best to blow up the kitchen with his crème brûlée. Can I call you back?"

"Sure, but maybe later in the week would be better. Things are crazy this evening and I have a lot of reading I have to do for the awards show."

Chapter Eleven

★

THE DRESS WAS FABULOUS, THE MOST BEAUTIFUL THING I'D EVER seen. It was way too expensive, but I fell in love with it the moment I tried it on in the ladies' room at *Juicy*. It had been messengered over with five other dresses from Heaven, Laura's favorite shop on Montana Avenue.

"I never thought I'd like you in that color, but I really do," Tracy said, giving me an appraising look. The dress was a soft metallic copper and reminded me of a gown Hilary Swank had worn on the red carpet. It wasn't something I would have chosen for myself, but Tracy was right, there was something special about it!

"It's not see-through, is it?" I said, twisting around to see myself in the bathroom mirror.

"I promise you it's not see-through," Tracy said with a laugh. "And it fits you perfectly. Honestly, Jess, this is the one. This is The Dress."

"I think you're right," I murmured, admiring the way the fabric fell sleekly over my shoulders and hugged my body. "It's going to be a shame to have to give it back after the show."

"Oh, what have we here? A private fashion show?" Alicia had slipped into the ladies' room and was eyeing my dress suspiciously.

"It's Jessie's dress for the Teen Choice Awards," Tracy babbled happily. "Doesn't she look beautiful? Really, Jess, people will think you're up for an award yourself!" I noticed the stricken look on Alicia's face and tried to catch Tracy's eye before she said another word. Was *Juicy* springing for a new dress for Alicia? From the expression on her face, the answer was no!

"I saw the delivery guy from Heaven, and I wondered what was going on," Alicia said slowly. "Do you normally get your clothes delivered to work?"

I flushed, wondering how to play down the whole dress thing, when Tracy sprang to my defense.

"This is business-related!" she said firmly. "Laura wanted Jess to have something nice to wear to the awards. After all, she's going to be standing on the red carpet for hours and she might end up being photographed herself."

I wriggled out of the dress, reaching for my blouse and skirt, wishing Alicia had never chosen that moment to walk into the ladies' room. Tracy, unfortunately, was making things worse with every word out of her mouth, and I knew the only thing was to get out of there fast.

"How nice," Alicia said nastily. "Nobody bothered to tell me we were getting free dresses for the event. Gee, what an oversight. I wish I had thought to ask for one. Guess you know more about getting these perks than I do."

"It's only a loan," I said quickly. "I'm giving it back right after the show." I sighed. I knew Alicia was going to hold this against me, no matter what I said. "And I didn't ask for it, it was Laura's idea. I don't think she even realized you were covering the event, or she'd have offered to do the same thing for you."

"Hmmm, guess it slipped her mind. Or maybe I'm not high enough up on the food chain around here to rate a free dress."

"Laura was rushing to go out of town, and I think it was an honest mistake," I insisted. I was pretty sure that was the case, and that Edgar had simply forgotten to tell Laura that he was sending Alicia along with me. Laura would certainly never go out of her way to antagonize Alicia, or do anything that would cause hurt feelings. But naturally Alicia would put the worst possible spin on things. "Let's go," I said to Tracy, who was helping me zip the dress back into the garment bag. I arched an eyebrow at Alicia, who was leaning against the sink with an evil smirk. "I need to cover the phones back in the editorial office."

THERE'S NO WAY TO EXPLAIN A HOLLYWOOD AWARD CEREMONY. As Tracy said, watching the crowd gather in the late-afternoon sunshine, "You have to see it to believe it." We arrived at the Dorothy Chandler Pavilion hours before the actual event, and I was surprised that there were hundreds of people already there ahead of us. Lights and electrical cables were strung along the edges of the famous red carpet, and cameramen and lighting technicians were guzzling bottled water as they joked back and forth, setting up their equipment. I recognized a few famous faces from television, and Giuliana DePandi smiled at me as she hurried by.

A crowd sat on bleachers overlooking the entrance to the pavilion and some couples even sat on blankets on the ground, as close to the rope line as they could get. The stars wouldn't be arriving for a few more hours, but the whole place was alive with energy, buzzing with noise and excitement. I was caught up in the moment, and could hardly believe that I was here in Hollywood, part of the whole amazing scene.

I'd been given a list of all the teen stars who were up for awards and a short bio of each. The "talent sheet" was overwhelming, everyone from Lindsay Lohan and Hilary Duff to singers like Christina Aguilera and Shakira.

"Did you really memorize all those bios?" Tracy asked, peering over my shoulder. "I'm impressed!" We had stepped into the shade and I was scanning the list, jotting down a few questions to ask each person. It was a blisteringly hot afternoon, and we both were wearing cotton skirts and sleeveless blouses. Our dresses were safely locked in the Wardrobe trailer and we planned on changing in another hour or two.

"Not all of them," I admitted. "I think I know enough about their movie and television credits, but I'm going to have trouble describing their outfits." Laura had e-mailed me with a reminder to be sure to discuss each star's gown as she paused for an interview.

"Don't worry about it," Tracy suggested. "Just tell them they look beautiful and ask them who designed their dress. That's what Melissa Rivers does all the time." She grinned. "If they don't know, that's their problem."

"Easy for you to say," I teased her. "You're not the one who's going to look like an idiot on national TV. But maybe you're right. They certainly should know who designed their dresses, shouldn't they? After all, they're getting them for free and they don't have to give them back, either!"

Joe, the cameraman, led me over to the spot where I was supposed to stand for my celeb interviews. My name was written in chalk on the concrete floor, and he explained that it was very important to stay at my assigned spot and not wander into anyone else's area. I nodded and thanked him. I had no intention of wandering into someone else's area; I would be rooted to my own spot, frozen in fear!

"Where's Alicia?" he said, checking a light meter. "I thought she was covering this with you."

"She had to go home to get some shoes, she'll be here any minute." I didn't want to say that Alicia had left the office in midmorning, determined to sneak home and relax and do her hair and nails for the big event.

The next couple of hours passed quickly and before we knew it, it was time to head to the Wardrobe trailer.

"Wonder what happened to Alicia?" Tracy said idly. "I can't believe she's still not here."

"Maybe she got tied up in traffic," I suggested. "Her boyfriend was supposed to drive her here and drop her off. Anyway, let's not worry about it. I just want to get to Wardrobe!"

I could hardly wait to put on my drop-dead-gorgeous dress. I was standing in my strapless bra and panties, trying to tame my heat-frizzed hair, when Tracy appeared with the zippered garment bag. "Do you want to put on your dress, or do you want to work on your hair some more?" she asked. She was teasing, but I knew I'd never get that long, silky Jennifer Aniston look, even if I spent half an hour with a flatiron.

"I'll have to pretend the curly look is in," I reminded her, as she unzipped the bag. "Ready for the dress!" I said happily.

There was a moment of silence and when I glanced at Tracy, she was staring into the garment bag, looking like she was ready to pass out. Her face was dead white, and her mouth formed an O like the figure in that Edvard Munch painting, but no sound was coming out. She looked up at me, her eyes enormous, shaking her head from side to side.

"Tracy, what is it? This is no time to kid around." I said a little impatiently. "Just give me the darn dress."

"I can't," she said in a strangled voice. "Something terrible has happened to it. It's ruined."

"What are you talking about?" I grabbed the garment bag

and nearly keeled over in shock when I saw my beautiful copper dress. It was hanging in shreds, as if a crazed killer had tried to hack it to death. "Oh, no!" I wailed. "What happened? Who could have done this?"

As I pulled the dress out of the bag, running my hand over the slashed fabric, a flash of bright yellow caught my eye. I lifted out Tracy's Indian-print sheath, the cute little dress she'd bought with Ellie on Melrose Avenue. "Your dress is ruined, too!"

"I know," she said miserably. "Why? Who would do this?"

Time stood still for a moment, and then Alicia emerged from the changing room, a sly smile squirming on her lips. "Oh, what have we here?" she said archly. "A wardrobe malfunction?"

Suddenly it all made sense to me. A lightbulb moment. Alicia's absence from the red carpet scene, her mysterious trip "home" to get her missing shoes, the snarky grin on her face as she fingered her tennis bracelet. If this was an episode of *CSI*, a pair of sharp investigators would find fibers from my dress on Alicia's clothing along with a pair of sharp scissors hidden in her Chanel clutch. They'd confront her, and she'd cave under tough interrogation, tearfully confessing to the crime.

But this was real life, not television, and Alicia was much too smart to implicate herself. After all, she had the presence of mind to destroy Tracy's dress as well, just in case I was tempted to borrow it! If that doesn't show the makings of a true evil genius, I don't know what does. But I knew we'd never prove it. I stood there, my mind scrambling for a solution, when Tracy grabbed her purse and raced to the door.

"Where are you going?" I said. I couldn't believe she was leaving me stranded in my bra and panties, with Alicia watching and loving every minute of it!

"Don't worry about anything," Tracy yelled. "I'll be right back." She shot a death glare at Alicia, who was calmly applying another layer of cocoa lip gloss, getting ready to face the cameras. "And don't let anyone take your place!" A final glare at Alicia and she was gone. I shook my head. Even Tracy couldn't save the situation this time; my night on the red carpet was falling apart!

Alicia flounced out the door a minute later, looking stunning in a pale-green silk shantung dress that set off her red hair. She turned at the door and gave me a fake sympathetic look. "So sorry that happened, sweetie. But don't worry, I can handle all the celebs you were supposed to interview. I can get the list from Joe. I'm sure he has a copy." She was so excited, she was tripping over her tongue, the words tumbling out haphazardly.

I felt my heartbeat speed up and a tightness build in me as she walked into the bright sunlight. Where was Tracy? If she had some plan B in mind, I would really like to know what it was! I was standing at the sink, my brow furrowed in genuine confusion, trying to make sense of the last five minutes. One minute I was ready to hit the red carpet, and now—nothing!

I was still standing there when to my amazement, Laura strolled in, talking on her cell phone. I had no idea she was even back in L.A., much less at the awards. She smiled at me and covered the mouthpiece for a second. "Nice job!" she said, her voice flattened to a whisper.

"What?" I said, baffled. I was standing half-naked in the Wardrobe trailer when I was supposed to be out interviewing stars on the red carpet. What in the world was she talking about?

She waved a copy of a glossy magazine in front of me. I recognized the *Juicy* logo on the cover. How could I have forgotten that today was the day the first issue was going to hit the stands? "Loved the article, Jess," she went on, apparently waiting for someone to come back on the line. "You really nailed it."

"My article?" I said blankly.

"The Jazz Holliday piece," Laura said, looking puzzled. "You did a terrific job. Edgar was very pleased with it; he even featured it on the cover. Haven't you seen it? Here, take my copy, I have more copies in the car." She paused. "It was a little rough in places, but nothing that some careful editing couldn't fix."

Then her face broke into a big grin and she said into the phone, "Peter, I'm here at the Dorothy Chandler Pavilion, where are you?" She moved toward the door, still talking, while I flipped through the pages.

There it was. My Jazz Holliday article, the one I never submitted. Someone must have taken my notes, the rough draft I had on my computer, and sent them to Laura while she was out of town. And Laura, unsuspecting, had whipped the article into shape and published it!

I scanned the first paragraph, feeling like I'd been punched in the gut. *"I'm so happy to have the lead in* Bad Intentions," *Jazz Holliday said, when interviewed in her beautiful Silver Lake condo. "All my hard work finally paid off!"* I didn't bother to read the rest; this was the kiss of death for Jazz and her television career. She would be devastated.

I leaned my hands against the cool porcelain sink, questions spinning around in my head like a tornado. Alicia had slashed my dress. Alicia had stolen my article and submitted it. Why? I shook my head, truly bewildered. *To make herself look good? To make me look like a total creep?* I sank my teeth into my lower lip the way I always do when I'm lost in thought. And then it came to me.

She knew what this would do to my relationship with Shane. Somehow she had discovered the Jazz–Shane relationship; it was all right there in my notes.

"I did the best I could!" Tracy said, flying into the trailer. "I know you're not crazy over beige, but it's a safe color and it's the right size." I nodded, staring at myself in the mirror, wondering how I could ever make this right. "Jessie!" she said impatiently, "snap out of it. Okay, so the dress looks like a piece of burned toast, but you have no choice. And I know it'll fit, it's just a straight sheath that hangs from the shoulders." She shot me a worried look. "Are you okay? Geez, a little gratitude would be nice! I told the taxi driver to take me to the nearest store and I made him double-park while I dashed inside."

"The dress is fine, Tracy," I said slowly, still lost in thought. "Thanks, really." I pulled off the tags and slipped the dress over my head, feeling Tracy's eyes boring a hole in my back. She deserved an explanation, but this wasn't the time to get into one. I jammed my feet into my heels and pushed my bangs out of my eyes. I had a job to do!

I darted to my spot just as Joe was moving in with the camera trained on Alicia. She saw me and paled. "You're here?" she gasped.

"I sure am!" I said, elbowing her aside. I thought I saw the hint of a smile on Joe's face, as Alicia nearly tottered over on her high heels. I had my notes in hand and was holding them inconspicuously, the way Laura had suggested. "Ready?" I asked Joe.

"Whenever you are."

The next two hours were a blur of famous faces, flashbulbs popping, fabulous clothes, and a few nerve-racking moments when I nearly didn't recognize certain stars. The parade was endless; some of the outfits were fabulous and some were fashion disasters. The fabulous ones included Gwen Stefani; Amber Tamblyn, who'd just finished making *Sisterhood of the Traveling Pants*; Fergie from the Black Eyed Peas; and Michelle Trachtenberg, the onetime Buffy sibling.

There were no glitches, no incidents like the Tara Reid Syndrome. (Lexi at work had told me that when the top of a star's dress nearly falls down at the *exact* moment the camera turns to her, it's called the Tara Reid Syndrome.) Some of the fashion choices were weird; a very famous starlet showed up in an over-sized tunic that would have looked better on Andre the Giant, and a top model was wearing a dress with scribbles all over it, as if she'd been mugged by a graffiti artist on the way to the awards.

I think I held up well, considering the stress of the mo-ment, and a few times Joe stuck his head around the camera to give me a big grin and a thumbs-up. It wasn't until the parade finally ended and I went back to the Wardrobe trailer to get my purse that I told Tracy about Alicia submitting the Jazz Holliday article. Just as I expected, she was outraged.

"I can't believe she'd pull something like that," she said in disbelief. "I mean I know Alicia is snarky and underhanded but what she did is truly evil." She paused. "Do you think anything can be done? Is it too late to save Jazz's career?"

I shook my head. "I don't know. I can go to Laura, but what good will that do? Even if she prints a retraction, it won't change anything. The damage is done, and anyway, the story happens to be true. So Edgar would probably never agree to a retraction."

Tracy was silent for a moment. "Ohmigosh," she said sud-denly. "What's going to happen with Shane? Has he heard about this? I thought you said Jazz only agreed to the interview be-cause he called her and asked her to do it."

"I'm sure he's heard about it, and he must be furious with me. Jazz trusted him, and he went out of his way to get the interview for me. And you know something, Tracy? I wasn't completely honest with him. I never told him that the whole idea was to get her to admit to being the lead actress in *Bad Intentions*. I acted like it was just another celeb profile." I splashed some cold water on my face and ran my hand through my hair. "You have no idea how much I regret doing that."

"We all do things we regret," Tracy said slowly. "But sometimes we have a chance to make them right."

"That's a nice thought, but I don't think it's going to happen this time," I told her. We left the trailer just as a huge influx of reporters came in to gather up their belongings. We were off for a round of parties, and I wasn't at all in a party mood.

WE HIT THREE PARTIES IN A ROW, AND I WAS HOBBLING UP THE Sunset Strip, my heels killing me, when I felt someone come up behind me and slip his arm around my waist. "Hey, you," a male voice said softly. "I was looking for you in the audience all night. It was hard to see with the lights, but I thought you might be standing somewhere in the back."

Shane! I wheeled around to face him, my heart hammering in my chest. I had waited for this moment all night. I had dreaded this moment all night! I knew that whatever happened in the next few minutes was going to change the whole course of my relationship with Shane and my life in Hollywood.

I took a deep breath and smiled at him. "No, I was stuck on the red carpet the whole time. I had back-to-back interviews and I never got a chance to get inside to see the show." As always, my heart did a little *ping* when I saw him. He was very tanned from his trip to Mexico, and his dark eyes were so bright they looked like they were lit from behind. We were stuck in a crush of partygoers waiting to go up the steps to Spago, the famous restaurant so popular with Hollywood A-listers. Joe, the cameraman, had taken a quick break to get another piece of equipment off the truck, and Tracy had suddenly disappeared, with no explanation.

I was alone with Shane, if you can be alone on a crowded sidewalk, being pushed from all sides, with photographers standing in the middle of the street taking pictures! There were so many celebrities, everywhere, that no one bothered Shane, no one called out his name as we linked hands, instinctively drawing closer to each other. They were too busy photographing the starlets in their filmy dresses. I looked up at him, captivated by the endless magic in his eyes. We were standing so close, I could feel the heat from his body. Even the air around him seemed charged with electricity.

"How did the interviews go?" He lowered his voice to a sexy whisper and gave my waist a gentle squeeze. "This must have been a big night for you."

"It's a big night for me right now," I said, feeling the sweep of his dark gaze. "This is the moment I was really waiting for, not the one on the red carpet." There. I was glad I put it out there. The attraction I felt for him was so strong, so undeniable that I wanted him to know about it, even if we could never be together, even if he could never forgive me for the Jazz Holliday piece.

"Me, too," he said in that husky drawl that always sent my pulse racing. "All I cared about tonight was seein' you again, Jessie. I would have called you, but I got in really late last night from Mexico." He ran his hand through his hair and I noticed that it was a little longer, and bleached even lighter from the sun. "Man, it was crazy down there. There were a couple of places that were so remote, around the Baja peninsula, that you could only get to them by boat. But I thought about you the whole time I was away, and a lot of things seem clearer to me now."

I swallowed hard as a thought suddenly hit me—maybe he hadn't even seen the *Juicy* article! Shane had just gotten back to town and hosted a major award show. Probably the last thing on his mind was sitting down and reading an entertainment magazine!

I couldn't go on another minute without clearing things up. Even if he didn't want anything to do with me, it was better to know right now.

"Shane," I said, trying to talk past the lump in my throat, "there's something I've got to tell you. Something happened while you were away—"

I didn't get any further, because he ran his thumb under my chin and gently tilted my face up to him. "I know all about it, Jess. The Jazz Holliday piece."

"You know about it!" I gasped.

Shane nodded, locking his fingers through mine more tightly as the line surged forward. "There was a message from Jazz when I got home late last night. Somehow she got an advance copy of the issue. She was pretty upset about it. Man, she sure wasn't expectin' that."

"Shane, it's not what it looks like," I said quickly. "I never would have betrayed Jazz. I wrote up the notes from the interview, but I never submitted the article. Someone else took the whole thing off my computer." Alicia's face, with her cold eyes and snarky little smile, drifted across my mind. "She's a co-worker at *Juicy*, and she's been out to get me since the first day. She wants to ruin everything for me," I said bitterly. *The big question was: had she succeeded?*

"I know all about that, Jess, Tracy told me." His magnetic eyes softened. "But I knew you would never have done anything like that, anyway. I figured something crazy had happened, some kind of a mistake, something out of your control." *So Tracy had told him the whole story?* Tracy's disappearance suddenly made sense to me.

"But what about Jazz?" I said miserably. "Is her career really over before it even begins?"

"No, we straightened everything out," he said, a faint smile teasing his mouth. "I called Norman and he got on it right away."

I was puzzled. Norman was Shane's agent. "But what can Norman do about it?"

"It turns out that the producers of *Bad Intentions* are the same producers for my new movie, and we're in the middle of some very delicate negotiations right now. So Norm told them that we'd really appreciate it if they would just let the whole *Juicy* thing slide, and not hold it against Jazz. After all, she didn't expect it to turn out this way, and she didn't mean to do anything wrong."

"And they agreed?" I was astounded. Sometimes the inner workings of Hollywood are beyond my comprehension.

"They sure did." He bent down and brushed his lips against mine for a gentle kiss, so quick it was almost subliminal. "Money talks in this town, Jess. Never forget that."

"I won't," I promised, even though money was the last thing on my mind at the moment. "So everything is okay? With us, I mean?"

"It's more than okay, Jess," Shane said. His eyes were dark and wickedly teasing. "Let's get out of this Spago party as soon as we can. I think I owe you a walk on the beach at Malibu, re-member? And this is the perfect night for it. There's a full moon up there, in case you hadn't noticed."

"I noticed," I said a little breathlessly. His mouth was close to mine and I wanted desperately to kiss him. I felt a little light-headed, nearly delirious with happiness. This was going to be the most exciting night of my life.

"Do you really have to go to Spago? Do you have any inter-views set up inside?" he murmured.

I shook my head. "Not really. Tracy was going to help Joe get some background shots, that's all. I already have way more material than they can ever use. Edgar just gave me a couple of invitations to the Spago party because he thought I'd enjoy mingling with all the stars."

"Mingle with the stars? Then let's forget about Spago and head straight to Malibu. You can mingle all you want with *this* star," he said devilishly. "Let's take that moonlit walk on the beach I promised you, Jess. One thing you should know about me, I'm a guy who always keeps his promises."

I smiled at him, a deep happy smile. "I certainly hope so," I told him.

Chapter Twelve

⭐

"SO WHAT'S GOING TO HAPPEN TO ALICIA?" TRACY AND I WERE SIT-ting at Frenchie's, a little outdoor café down by the Santa Monica Pier, the next morning. "Please don't tell me she's going to keep her job after what happened."

It was a beautiful day, and the Pacific shimmered a pale aquamarine, dusted with a sprinkling of whitecaps. *I wish I could stay here forever*, I thought, watching a flock of seagulls sweep across the cloudless sky. California has an energy and excitement I've never seen anyplace else, and I wondered if I could talk my mom into relocating her antiques business to the West Coast. The trouble is, she's pure New England, through and through. I wanted to close my eyes and soak up some white-hot rays, but I knew Tracy was waiting for an answer.

"Okay," I quipped, "I won't tell you she's going to keep her job." I gave Tracy a deadpan stare and drummed my fingers on the glass-topped table, waiting for her reaction. Tracy is as predictable as a volcano, and just as volatile.

She didn't disappoint me. "No!" she said, plunking both elbows down on the table so hard she nearly upset her double cappuccino. "No way! That can't be true. Not after what she did to you and Jazz. She almost ruined both your careers and she gets off scot-free?" She leaned across the table, her eyes wide, her voice quivering with indignation. "That's got to be the craziest thing I ever heard of!"

"Sorry, Trace. I was surprised too, if that's any consolation."

She stared at me for a long moment and then folded her arms across her chest and collapsed back in the chair, suddenly deflated, like a popped balloon. "I just don't believe it," she said in a wobbly voice. "If she stays at *Juicy*, that means there's no justice in the world."

I made a derisive noise. "Welcome to the real world, Trace," I said wearily. "Things are never what they seem, especially in Tinseltown, remember? And you know what they say—if you want justice, you better watch Court TV, because you're not gonna find it in La-La Land."

"So she'll be back at work on Monday? That's it?" Tracy bit her lower lip, her blue eyes clouding with disappointment.

Funny, she seemed to be taking the news harder than I had, but I'd had more time to think about it. The rage that was boiling in my stomach last night had slowed to a simmer, and I was calmer, ready to face the cold hard facts in front of me.

"It looks that way. She's staying put, at least for the time being, and we'll be working side by side as usual. Laura called me last night on my cell when I was out with Shane and filled me in on the game plan."

Some game, I thought. Alicia stole my article and slashed my dress, but the score was still Alicia 1, Jessie 0. What did they call it? A zero-sum game? Go figure. If I tried to make sense of it all, I would drive myself crazy.

"So that's how it happened, then? Laura blew the whistle on her?"

"She sure did. That's when things really hit the fan. Laura heard what happened in the Wardrobe trailer from some of the other reporters and went to Edgar with all the gruesome details. She told him everything Alicia had done, stealing the Jazz Holliday notes off my computer, submitting them with my byline, slashing our red carpet dresses . . ."

I let my voice trail off, remembering how surprised I'd been to get that phone call from Laura, her voice so low and hushed that I'd had to jam my cell phone smack against my ear to hear her. And Shane had stood next to me, his handsome face frowning, holding me very lightly around the waist. He knew it was an emotional moment for me and I was happy he'd been there with me.

Laura had seemed embarrassed at the unfairness of it all, but it was obvious that she wasn't the person in charge of Alicia's fate. And she wasn't really personally involved, like I was. She didn't have anything emotionally at stake in whether Alicia lost her job or stayed at the magazine, so she just stuck to the facts.

I think she was concerned that I'd been treated badly—but only up to a point. Laura has a fantastic job at *Juicy*, and she certainly wasn't going to tell Corporate how to handle personnel decisions. I had the feeling she was calling me out of courtesy, or that maybe someone had told her to give me a ring. (Maybe Edgar?)

Even though Laura realized I had gotten the short end of the stick, she still wasn't going to go out on a limb to make sure Alicia was punished. Why? Who knows? Maybe she figured no real damage was done, since Shane had stepped in to make sure Jazz's career was safe. All's well that ends well?

So, in the end, *Juicy* was going to take the line of least resistance and keep Alicia's father happy. Alicia had gotten the magazine internship because of family connections, and she was obviously going to keep her job, the same way.

After all, as they say on *The Apprentice*, "It's not personal, it's just business." And I was beginning to think that lies, backstabbing, and deceit were business as usual in Hollywood.

Somehow there didn't seem to be any point in rehashing all this in the bright California sunshine. The day was too perfect, the air too balmy, and talking about Alicia was such a buzzkill! But Tracy wanted to know the facts and one thing I can say about my best friend—she's relentless.

"Just explain something to me," Tracy demanded. "Once Laura spilled the beans to Edgar, what happened? Why didn't he go ballistic? I can't imagine Edgar letting someone get away with what she did. Even if he wasn't upset by the dresses, you'd think he'd nail her for grabbing your feature off the computer and turning it in." She gave a little snort. "There's gotta be a section on that in the employee handbook. They even forbid chewing gum in the halls at *Juicy!* What about sabotage? Shouldn't that be grounds for dismissal?"

I bit back a sigh and shrugged. "Tracy, I'm telling you, you just have to let go of this, because nothing is really going to happen to Alicia. She'll get a slap on the wrist, a little reprimand, that's all. There's no sense in making yourself crazy over it, at least that's what I've decided. Everything I've told you is confidential, by the way. The only people who know what really happened are Laura, Edgar, and a couple of people in Human Resources."

"I still can't believe she's going to be at the magazine." She gave a delicate little shudder. "I'll have to see her at lunch every day. I don't think I can just sit there and pretend none of this really happened."

"Tell me about it," I said sarcastically. "I'll have to see her all day long. But that's the bottom line—she's still got her summer internship. None of this will probably even show up on her record. She'll be passed off to her next employer as a little gem, a real go-getter, complete with a sparkling résumé."

We were silent for a moment, staring at a group of bronzed surfers soaring across the waves, their surfboards glinting off the emerald sea. California guys, waiting to catch the next wave.

"I wonder what really happened," Tracy murmured. "You know, the real story. Did money change hands, or does Alicia know everybody's secrets? Did she threaten to blackmail Edgar, or maybe Laura?" Tracy's mouth twisted sardonically. "There's got to be some dirty laundry that she's threatening to expose; why else would they keep her?"

"It's not that," I said flatly. I waited while the incredibly buff waiter—a struggling actor, no doubt—refilled our coffee cups and flashed us a blinding smile before edging away. "Here's the bottom line. Alicia's dad is a partner with Edgar—he's one of the original investors."

"Ah, the money man. I had forgotten about that." Tracy looked a little wistfully after the waiter as he strolled away. In a town full of great-looking guys, she hadn't met anybody she found interesting enough to date.

"Exactly. Money talks. Not just here in Los Angeles, but everywhere."

Tracy nodded somberly. "So we may never know exactly what happened."

I laughed. "You sound like something out of *Cold Case*."

Tracy grinned, and I figured we both could put the Alicia

incident behind us for the rest of the day. I'd find out about the fallout for my own career when I went into work the next day.

My cell rang just then, blaring out a soft rock version of "Call Me the Breeze." Tracy's eyebrows shot up, and I grinned.

"Shane changed my ringtone," I explained. I'd been teasing Shane that you can take the boy out of the country, but you can't take the country out of the boy, and the next thing you know, I had a new ringtone. The sweet sounds of Shakira had morphed into Lynyrd Skynyrd's southern rock. Shane said he wanted to make sure that every time my cell rang, I would smile and think of him!

My pulse picked up when I heard Shane's hot sexy voice glide over the wire. "Hey baby, just wanted to say I was thinking about you," he said, catching me off guard. "Last night was awesome, you know? I can't get you out of my head, Jess."

"It was quite a night for me, too," I stammered. I could feel a warm flush starting to creep up my neck, and decided to keep the conversation on neutral topics. Tracy locked eyes with me, but I wasn't giving anything away. "What are you up to?" I asked him.

Shane sighed. "Boring stuff. Meetings all day, mostly with Adriana about PR events. She's got this long list of requests, some are from people who just want a photo op with me, or a meet and greet. But then there's a mountain of invitations to industry dinners and awards shows. The kind of thing that can take up a whole evening. They're a real snooze, unless you're with the right person, of course."

Adriana. I flashed back to the night when we'd nearly been mobbed by the paparazzi at the Blue Lotus. I'd been so shaken up, I'd asked Shane to take me straight home. I've learned a lot about Hollywood since then, and I knew I'd handle the situation differently this time. I'd stand my ground and wouldn't run for cover like a frightened little rabbit.

Shane's deep baritone dragged back to the present. "Maybe you'd like to come to some of them with me? I'll let them snap a few pictures and then we can cut out early and spend some time together. All I really have to do is put in an appearance, no one cares how long I stay."

I thought for a minute. It would be so easy to say yes, but everything was different now that I was working for *Juicy*. I might be Shane's girlfriend—on some level—but I was also a reporter. Had he forgotten that? I certainly hadn't.

Edgar had very strict ideas about mixing business with pleasure, and I wasn't sure how he'd react to seeing me turn up at an affair with Shane. Plus the stars might not be too thrilled about having a journalist in their midst. Even though the whole incident with Jazz had been smoothed over, I wondered if some people in town were suspicious of me and figured I couldn't be trusted. If they didn't know the full story about the Jazz Holliday piece, they probably were thinking the worst. After all, Hollywood is a town built on gossip, and one rumor, one lie, one misstep can ruin your reputation.

It would never occur to them that Alicia had masterminded the whole thing. I wondered if that little tidbit had been left out of the gossip that was making the rounds? I figured Jazz would tell people what really happened, but sometimes half-truths take on a life of their own, and if I'd never left those notes on my computer, Alicia couldn't have swiped them.

I even wondered if I'd snare any more good assignments at the magazine, or if I'd be relegated to some low-level job like filing or fact checking. After all, if the publicists decided they didn't trust me and didn't want me anywhere near their star clients, what could Edgar do? It might be that my days of doing star profiles were over, and now I'd be covering routine industry functions with a general press pass.

Maybe none of this had occurred to Shane? I'd better be up front with him, I decided. I had to do what was best for my career, and not do anything to jeopardize it. As far as I knew, I was holding on by my fingernails at *Juicy*.

"The thing is, Shane," I said slowly, "I think it would be better if we go separately to any kind of entertainment event from now on. I might get the chance to cover the stars for *Juicy* and I don't want it to look like there's any conflict of interest. Just think," I teased him, "the next time you walk out of a premiere, I could be standing there waiting for you, with a mike held up in your face. Just like Nancy O'Dell."

"Man, I hadn't thought of that," Shane said. "I'd rather have you there as my date, instead of having you ask twenty questions." I heard a muffled conversation in the background, and then, "Gotta run, Jess. They want to do some publicity pictures and I've got to get changed. I'll call you about next weekend, okay? I'd like to show you some more of my favorite spots out here."

"Sounds good. Talk to you later." I clicked off my cell and looked at Tracy. "I think Shane and I finally got some things settled."

"Are things with Shane ever really settled?" Tracy asked.

I bit back a sigh. "As much as they can be," I said after a moment. Tracy was right, I decided. There was always something tentative about my relationship with Shane, a missing piece of the puzzle.

An hour later, we were strolling along the boardwalk when someone whizzed up behind me on in-line skates. I started to move out of the way, edging over to the right, when I felt a gentle tap on my shoulder.

"Jessie, I'm so glad I caught up with you. I tried to call you at Ellie's and she said you were havin' breakfast down by the beach. I figured I'd just zip on down here and talk to you."

"Jazz," I said, feeling a wave of embarrassment crash over me. "I was going to call you from work tomorrow." As soon as the words were out of my mouth, I realized what a lame excuse that was. I'm a terrible liar, and I'm afraid it shows.

The truth was I'd been dreading this moment and wondered where to begin. I knew Shane had told Jazz I wasn't responsible for the article being published, but I still felt sorry for all the problems I had caused her. Guilt plucked at me because if I'd never interviewed her (or if I'd been more suspicious of Alicia), none of this would have happened. I noticed Tracy had edged over to a T-shirt shop, pretending to flip through some piles of tie-dyes. "I can't tell you how sorry I am about everything. You see, the whole thing started when Alicia—"

"That's okay, sweetie," she cut in smoothly. "I know all about Alicia. Shane told me what happened. Back in Texas, we'd call her a snake in the grass, plus a few other things," she added with a pussycat smile. She looked sensational in a black spandex halter top and biker pants, her thick blond hair hanging down her back in a long braid. People turned to stare at her, even in Santa Monica where all the girls look like supermodels.

"But I still feel terrible," I said, thinking how upset Jazz must have been, and how she must have thought I'd betrayed her. "I wish I could make it up to you."

"There's nothin' to make up, I swear," she said, her Texas twang sweet as honey. "It's not your fault *Juicy* hired someone like that. There's no way in the world you could have predicted what that girl would do." She paused. "As far as makin' it up to me, I do have one request, sugar." Her wide eyes were teasing, tantalizing.

"Sure," I said quickly, "what is it?"

"Well, now that the cat is out of the bag on *Bad Intentions*, the producers are plannin' on a bash to end all bashes. It's gonna be at the Bev next month, and they're pullin' out all the stops. How about if I sent over a bunch of invitations to the gang at *Juicy*? Just to show there's no hard feelin's?"

"That would be awesome," I said. "I bet everyone would love to go." Did she mean she wanted me to cover the event for

Juicy? But she said *invitations*, so maybe that wasn't what she had in mind at all. If she wanted me there as a guest, I'd have to rethink everything I'd just told Shane.

"And I want you there as my personal guest," Jazz said, her green eyes wide and serious. "Reporters are a dime a dozen out here. But this is the kind of town where a girl really needs a friend, you know?"

Did I ever! "You're absolutely right on that one," I assured her. "And I'm flattered that you think of me as a friend, Jazz. Sure, I'd love to go." Not only was it a really nice thing for her to do, it would also restore my reputation in Hollywood if the celebs saw the two of us together.

"Oh and by the way, another friend is coming, too," she said in her lilting Texas accent. "I think he's a pretty good friend of yours, as well. Shane Rockett."

I felt a silly little rush of pleasure that warmed me all the way down to my toes. Was Shane my friend? Or something else? Just hearing his name made my heart give a funny little lurch. "Thank you, Jazz," I said. "We'll be there."

It was late afternoon when Tracy and I finally got back to Ellie's. Tracy was on the balcony, flipping through a fashion magazine, and Ellie was busy in the kitchen, throwing together a vegetarian pasta dish for dinner.

I knew it was time to do something I had been agonizing over. It was time to call Marc! I'd promised him we'd talk later in the week, but somehow the whole disaster with Alicia had put it right out of my mind. Or was I just looking for an excuse not to call him? Was I still trying to decide what I wanted to do?

I sighed, figuring out the time difference between California and New Orleans. It was eight in the evening in New Orleans, a good time to call Marc, because they didn't serve dinner at the Black Swan on Sundays. They put out a big brunch from noon to five and then the kitchen was closed for the day, so Marc would probably be chillin', as he liked to say. My heart hammered when I asked myself the real question that was bothering me—what would I say to him?

Nothing with Marc was simple. Every time I thought I'd figured out our relationship, there seemed to be a new twist to the story, and I felt like I was back at square one. But I couldn't put off calling him for another minute. I still didn't know what I'd say, and I could only hope that the right words would come to me.

"Jessie!" His voice was like white lightning, full of energy and pumped with excitement. "I had the feeling you'd call tonight, I really did. Hold on a sec, I need to turn this down." I heard some blues music pounding in the background and it quickly melted into a low hum. "There, that's better," he said.

"B. B. King?" I asked.

"Good guess. He's the best." A little pause, then, "I saw you on the red carpet, Jessie; you looked beautiful. In fact, the whole staff watched the awards show; everybody stayed glued to the television waiting for your interviews. You looked more beautiful than the stars up there with their awards, and that's the truth, *cherie*."

I laughed. Marc was always good for my ego, maybe too good! "That's nice of you to say, Marc, but believe me, out here in Hollywood, I'm nothing special. I'm sort of like a minnow swimming in a sea of—"

"In a sea of sharks," Marc jumped in. "I've heard Hollywood is a tough town, Jessie, and I wondered how you'd survive out there. I've been worried about you," he added, his voice taking on a husky tone. "I really wonder if you belong out there, and sometimes I just wish you'd stayed in Bedford for the summer."

"It hasn't always been easy," I said ruefully. "But somehow I'm getting through it. And I've got Tracy out here with me, so that really helps. I've learned one thing, Marc. This is the kind of town where you really need a good friend," I said, echoing Jazz's feelings.

"But you've got one—me!" Marc insisted. "You know, I can be out there for you in a flash, Jessie. Just say the word and I'll jump on the next plane." I flinched, thinking that having Marc in town would only add another layer of complications to my life.

He obviously wanted to see me, but did I really want to see him when things were so uncertain? The last thing I wanted to do was hurt Marc, but things were still up in the air between us. Shane had stolen his way into my heart, into my life, and things would never be the same.

"I appreciate that," I told him, "but there really isn't much you could do to help at the moment, Marc. Most of my problems are related to my internship at the magazine, you know, business stuff." *Backstabbing, lies, betrayal*, I added silently. Just business, Hollywood-style.

There was no point in getting into the stolen article or my ongoing battle with Alicia. Marc couldn't help me with any of that, and knowing Marc, he'd be worried sick about me. Deep down, I knew that whatever happened, Marc would always be on my side of any battle. That's just the way he is, always loyal to his friends.

"So things at this magazine, *Juicy*, they're going well?" Marc had this sexy New Orleans accent, like Dennis Quaid in *The Big Easy*. He was fluent in French, and from time to time a touch of his Cajun ancestry showed through in the slow rhythms of his speech.

"It's going really well. I've had some tough moments here and there, but nothing I can't handle. It's an awesome opportunity for me, Marc, and it's the best summer job anyone could ever hope to have. Sometimes I walk into the lobby at *Juicy* and can't believe that I'm really part of such a cool magazine. It's hard to believe that things can change so fast, and all because of a glitch on that audio track."

Marc was silent for a moment, as if he was weighing his words carefully. "Sometimes change comes when we least expect it, Jessie. My whole summer has changed, too. You know,

I'd planned on you spending some time down here with me. In fact, my whole family was counting on it." He gave a low chuckle. "They love you, you know."

"I love them, too," I told him. I meant every word. Marc's family was amazing and I had gotten really friendly with his mother when I was staying in New Orleans last summer.

"But . . . ?" He left the word hanging, and I took a deep breath. This would be the tough part.

"But I don't think I'll be getting down to see you, after all, Marc. Not this summer, anyway." The words came out in a rush, as if they were being pulled out of me, and now there was no way I could take them back. The moment I spoke, I knew I had done the right thing, because I felt an immediate sense of relief. But that was quickly followed by a tug of guilt as I heard a soft intake of breath on the other end of the line.

"I was afraid that's what you were going to say, Jessie." He was silent for a moment, and I bit my lip, wondering what was going to happen next. "And it's not really because you're too busy. It's not about the pressure of work, is it?"

"No," I admitted in a quavery voice. "It's a lot more than that. I don't know how to explain it, Marc," I began, "but things have just gotten so complicated. Nothing is simple like it was when I was down in New Orleans." I felt hot tears stinging the back of my eyelids, threatening to spill down my cheeks, and I bit down hard on my lower lip. This was no time for a crying jag; it would just make the situation worse.

"You don't have to explain anything to me," Marc said after a long moment. "I've been thinking a lot about you, Jessie, and I think I finally get the picture."

"You do?"

"This is the way I see it, *cherie*. You have a life out there in Hollywood, and an exciting career that means a lot to you. You've worked hard, and you deserve all the good things that have come your way. I'd have to be crazy not to realize that."

"Well, that's part of it," I said hesitantly. "My summer internship really is the chance of a lifetime, Marc. It's very important to me." I didn't tell him that I hoped the internship wouldn't end when the summer was over, and that maybe I could persuade Mom to move out here.

"And there's a guy out there who's important to you, too. A guy whose name is a household word all over the world—Shane Rockett."

"About that—" I tried to jump in and do a little damage control, but Marc wasn't going to let me.

"No, *cherie*, don't say a word," he said firmly. "I've seen the two of you together, Jessie. I'd be a fool if I didn't realize how much you two feel about each other. It comes across in the pictures, you know. The camera doesn't lie." An image of Shane flew into my mind. Marc was right. The chemistry between us is so incredible, it seemed to jump right off the page when I looked at those tabloid shots.

But my spirits wilted a little, because I knew how hard it must be for Marc to admit this, even if it was painfully obvious to him. Funny, I never thought he'd be the one to lay it all out on the line, and I felt like a first-class coward. I was the one who couldn't face facts, not Marc.

"Well, it's not quite that simple," I said, still not willing to admit the obvious.

"No, you're wrong, Jess. I'm afraid it really is simple," Marc said, with a sad little laugh. "You're the most amazing girl I've ever met, but I can't compete with a movie star. And I don't feel like sharing you anyway. I'm just not that kind of guy. There's somebody out there who's right for me, just like you've found someone who's right for you."

A long pause while my thoughts scattered through my head like dry leaves across the sidewalk on a windy day. "I think you're a wonderful guy," I said softly. "I wish things had turned out differently, but you're right. Shane and I do have something special together." I waited, but he was silent. "So where does that leave us?" I asked finally. "I always want you to be part of my life, you know that."

"And I want you in my life, *cherie*," he told me. "So do you think you have room in your life for a really good friend?"

I smiled past the lump in my throat. "I'll always have room in my life for a friend like you, Marc. Always."

Chapter Thirteen

★

"SO THAT'S THE WAY YOU LEFT IT? THE TWO OF YOU ARE JUST going to be friends?"

"Good friends. Marc is too nice a guy; I just couldn't keep him dangling on the string anymore, and this way everything is out in the open." It was the next morning, and Tracy and I were rushing across the lobby of *Juicy* hoping to get to the doors of the packed elevator before they swooshed closed. Edgar is big on punctuality, and the last thing I wanted to do was be late on my first day back after "the incident."

"Speaking of out in the open, I wonder what Alicia will have to say for herself?" Tracy panted as we raced across the pink marble tiles.

"I have no idea," I said, feeling my stomach clench with

nerves. "It would be great if she just wouldn't show up today, but I don't think I'm going to be that lucky."

"I want a full report," Tracy said. "Call me if you get a second, otherwise I'll see you at lunch at twelve."

We darted inside just as the elevator doors were closing, and I breathed a sigh of relief.

I'd tried to mentally prepare myself for seeing Alicia, but I wasn't sure if I'd ever be ready to confront her. Every time I thought about her betrayal, my guts twisted, like someone had just sucker-punched me in the solar plexus. Would she be embarrassed to see me? Would she even bother to apologize? I had no idea. Alicia was a wild card at best; at worst, a "snake in the grass," as Jazz had said.

The moment we stepped out onto the eighth floor, I ran smack into Edgar. "I'd like to see you in my office, Jessie," he said in his clipped style. "Fifteen minutes sharp." He barely broke his stride as he hurried down the maze of corridors to his corner office.

"I'll be there," I gulped.

"Wow, he looked grim. Wonder what that's all about?" Tracy muttered. "I'll get down to the art department so you can get yourself together."

I nodded, already speed-walking toward my office. I automatically looked at my watch again. Fourteen minutes and counting! I went through a mental checklist of everything I had to do the moment I hit my desk. Check my e-mail, run through my voice mail messages, and one more little detail—try to stop my heart from hammering its way out of my chest! Was this the end of my career at *Juicy*? Was Edgar going to tell me to pack up my things? It looked like this was the moment of truth—the question is, was I ready for it?

"Have a seat, Jessie," Edgar said a few minutes later. He looked dapper as ever in a navy blue pinstripe suit and a red "power" necktie as he motioned me to a black leather club chair. He perched on the edge of his impressive desk, his eyes thoughtful. "Well," he said, smiling ruefully, "last week was quite a week for you, wasn't it? Who would have thought your introduction to Hollywood would be so—" he paused, glancing at a message light flickering on his phone— "shattering."

"It was a surprise to me," I said slowly. "And you're right, it was shattering. That's the perfect word for it." *But luckily I didn't give Alicia the satisfaction of seeing me fall into pieces!*

"I talked to Laura, you know, and she told me everything," he went on. "She said you handled yourself very well during the whole ordeal with Alicia. And Tracy did an exemplary job, too, from what I heard. I'm very impressed at her ingenuity, running out to buy you a dress to replace the one that had been destroyed. Very quick thinking, indeed."

Destroyed? Interesting the way he skipped over Alicia's part in all this, I thought. "Tracy saved the day," I agreed. "I don't think it would have occurred to me to buy a new dress at the last minute. I think I was in shock."

"Of course you were," he said sympathetically. "Anyone would be. But you did manage to pull yourself together and do an excellent job for us out on the red carpet. I reviewed the tapes over the weekend and I liked the questions you asked. You seemed very poised and relaxed on camera. No one would have suspected all the drama and intrigue going on backstage."

I shrugged. "I knew I had to get out there and do my best."

"Well, good work at *Juicy* gets rewarded, Jess, and I just wanted you to know that you'll be getting some top-notch assignments from now on."

"I will?" I blurted out. Up until this second, I wasn't sure if I'd been tainted somehow by the whole Alicia affair and thought that my stock at *Juicy* might have plummeted.

"Absolutely. And so will Tracy. I'm meeting with her supervisor today to make sure she gets some first-rate photography assignments." He paused, splaying his fingers on the desk. "As for Alicia . . . I'm sure you're wondering what's going to happen to her."

"The question crossed my mind, yes." I took a deep breath, wondering if she'd be fired after all.

"Alicia's staying, Jessie. For a variety of reasons that I'm not at liberty to discuss." He ran his fingers over his appointment book and for the first time, Edgar looked a little uncomfortable. I knew what he meant by "a variety of reasons." Investment money in the magazine, dollars and cents. A real no-brainer.

Then came the good news. "But there's one small change," he added, locking eyes with me. "Small, but I think it will make your life a little easier. Alicia won't be working side by side with you anymore." My relief must have shown on my face because he allowed himself a tiny smile. "She's leaving Editorial and going to work in the archives."

"The archives? But *Juicy* doesn't have an archives department yet."

"Very perceptive of you to notice that," Edgar said in a teasing voice. "We don't have an archives department yet, but we will. Alicia will be setting up some files in the basement offices. She can do a little research here and there, and then as the issues go to press, she can enter the articles into the system for us."

So Alicia was relegated to the basement! I could hardly believe my luck. Things were working out better than I had hoped. With any luck, I wouldn't have to see her at all.

"So . . . I just wanted to make sure you understood the situation, before I wrote a memo outlining the staffing changes. I wanted you to be the first to know, in light of . . . everything that's happened." He eased himself off the desk and edged toward the door, indicating the meeting was over.

"I appreciate your telling me all this, Edgar." I slid out of my seat, and he gave me a warm handshake, his eyes icy and piercing.

"You have a great future with us, Jessie," he said warmly. "Never forget that. The sky's the limit for you."

I DRIFTED BACK TO MY OFFICE, STILL DAZED BY EDGAR'S COMments, wrapped in a happy glow. The door to Editorial was open and I spotted Alicia tossing some files into a cardboard box. When she saw me she looked up with a scowl, her face flushed. I had the feeling she'd been crying because her eyes seemed unnaturally bright and her nose was bright pink. The box started to overbalance on the edge of the desk and I rushed forward to steady it.

"Can I help you with that?"

"I'm fine, thanks," she said, sneering as she snatched the box away from me. Up close, I could see tiny tear tracks on her face. "I'm making my getaway, in case you hadn't noticed."

"Getaway?"

She gave a dismissive wave. "From Editorial. From the eighth floor." She looked me up and down with a cold stare. "Saying adios to all the little office drones." So this was how she was going to play it, right up until the end, I thought. "From now on, I'm on special assignment."

"Well, good luck with your uh, special assignment." She gave me a swift look to see if I was being sarcastic and then she flashed a breezy smile.

"I'm really looking forward to it. A brand-new position, head of special projects. And they chose me! I'll be working closely with Edgar and all the top executives. It's a tough job, but I know I'm up for it."

I nodded. "I'm happy for you, I really am." And I meant it. She brushed past me and for some reason, I reached out and touched her arm. "Alicia," I said slowly, "good luck with everything, okay?"

"I don't need luck, sweetie," she said smoothly. "I have something you'll never have—talent."

Ouch! The same old Alicia; some things never change. She tightened her grip on the box, took one last look at her empty desk, and headed out the door.

I settled into my chair, took a deep breath, and called Tracy to fill her in. She wanted a play-by-play description and at the end, she let out a low whistle. "So it all worked out okay in the end."

"I think so," I agreed, "She's still here, but she's not in my hair, and there's nothing she can do to screw things up for me again. We're nine floors apart, and with any luck, we won't even run into each other."

The morning passed quickly, and I was surprised how peaceful the office was without Alicia's constant barbs and negativity. I answered my e-mail, took a dozen phone calls from publicists who wanted me to interview their clients, and managed to tackle my mountain of filing. I even took some time to put together some ideas to pitch at the weekly editorial meeting. If I was still in the game at *Juicy*, I decided, I might as well play to win. And the way to score points at *Juicy* was to come up with great story ideas.

It was nearly twelve when the phone rang, and I picked it up, without taking my eyes off the computer screen.

"Editorial," I murmured, staring at a list of candidates for next year's VMAs.

"Hey, baby." *Shane!*

"Hey yourself," I said, my pulse picking up a notch. Just the sound of his sexy voice could turn my heart sideways. "What's up?"

"You know how I planned on seein' you this weekend, and showing you some sights around town?" His voice was a little muffled as if he were talking on his cell.

"I remember." As if I could forget!

"Can't do it," he said in that smoky drawl. "Change of plans."

A beat passed while my mind raced, trying to take in the disappointing news. Change of plans? That could mean anything. Was he canceling our date? Postponing it? Was I back to square one with him? My heart hammered at the thought of being stood up by Shane Rockett one more time, but this time I wasn't going to put up with it.

"Why can't you do it?" I demanded. "What kind of change of plans?" The old Jessie would have caved, played the nice-girl card, and let him off the hook without an explanation or an apology. But times had changed, and I figured if I survived the Alicia incident, I could handle anything that Hollywood—or Shane Rockett—threw my way.

He laughed. "Wow, you're soundin' mighty spunky today, Jess. Mighty spunky, indeed."

"Yes, I'm feeling mighty spunky, as you say," I said icily. "You were saying . . ."

"I was sayin' that I can't wait till the weekend to see you," he said, his voice suddenly sounding louder over the wire. "And that even though I know you're busy, sittin' at that computer, I'm goin' to whisk you away for lunch. Today. Right this minute. You're lookin' cute as a button, by the way. Love that red skirt."

"Cute as a button, what are you—oh!" I turned to see Shane lounging in the doorway, looking movie-star cool in his shades and boots. "I can't believe you're here," I said, which has got to be one of the most idiotic comments I've ever made. I pushed back my chair and stood up awkwardly, smoothing my skirt, while he pulled off his shades to take a better look. Apparently he liked what he saw because his famous grin widened.

"I told you, babe, I couldn't wait. I just had to see you today." The trademark cocky smile, the edgy confidence, a full blast of the Shane Rockett magic hit me square between the eyes.

A secretary passing by in the corridor peeked in, raised her eyebrows, and then flashed me a "is that who I think it is" look. I motioned her to come on inside, but she scurried away, face flushed, probably eager to broadcast the news to the rest of the building.

"But I can't have lunch with you today, Shane. I've already made plans with Tracy—we're getting together at noon." I glanced at my watch. She'd be expecting me down in the cafeteria any minute and I wasn't going to ditch her, not for a megastar like Shane, not for anyone. I'd learned a lot about loyalty and friendship in the last forty-eight hours and I knew that Tracy was the one person who would always be there for me, no matter what. Shane, however tempting, would have to wait.

"Relax, Jess, it's okay," Tracy piped up. She'd appeared out of nowhere, ducked under Shane's arm, and scooted into my office. "You're not deserting me. Shane invited me to come along, isn't that cool? And guess what, we don't have to rush right back to work, so we can make a whole afternoon of it."

"We can?"

"I've already cleared it with Edgar," Shane said. "Here's the deal, Jessie. Edgar decided you needed a little treat after everything you've been through, so we're headin' down to Venice for a nice lunch on the water. He even said to take as much time as we want. It's his way of saying he appreciates you, I guess."

I stood up, my knees wobbly. "I don't know what to say."

"You don't need to say anything." Shane flashed his famous grin. "Just grab your shades and let's go, girl. It's a sunny day and time's a-wastin'. We're standin' here talkin' and burnin' daylight, as we say back in Dallas."

Tracy groaned at his down-home expression. "I thought you were gonna say, 'and the catfish are bitin'.'"

"Well, that too," Shane teased her right back. "I didn't know you knew that expression, Tracy. You're beginnin' to sound like a Texas girl, through and through. You'll have to teach Jessie here how to talk Texan when you get the chance."

A few minutes later, all three of us walked out the double doors into the brilliant California sunshine. Shane had parked his silver Jag right in front of the *Juicy* offices, nestled in between a candy apple–red Porsche and a lemon-yellow Rolls. I glanced down the wide expanse of Wilshire Boulevard, taking in the glitzy boutiques, the towering skyscrapers, and the noonday crush of gorgeous people rushing out to their power lunches.

I was here in Hollywood and I was part of it all! I could hardly believe my good luck. The whole summer stretched out before me, and I didn't think life could get any better than this. Never, in my wildest dreams, did I think I'd end up with an awesome job, an amazing best friend, and a movie-star boyfriend who just happened to be the sexiest teen star in the world.

And it's all happening to me, Jessie Phillips, from Bedford, Connecticut. I nearly pinched myself to make sure I wasn't dreaming. Pretty incredible, right? It was true what Shane said. Hollywood is a magical place and exciting things can happen when you least expect them.

I gave a big happy sigh. This was going to be the best summer of my life, no doubt about it.